No Landscape

Lasts Forever

D1557486

A few words about the writer, Amber Colleen Hart

A number of years ago, as I was creating The Writer's Loft at Middle Tennessee State University (now MTSU-WRITE), I knew that there would be a day when I would no longer be a part of that program, but I would pop open a book, or newspaper, or magazine one lazy afternoon in my home and see some of the good work that was being done by both students and mentors in the program. Indeed, I had that privilege when I read Amber Hart's short story collection. *No Landscape Lasts Forever.* The prose is beautiful, and Ms. Hart's syntax is perfect for her characters. Within each story, I appreciate her ability to celebrate empathy in her characters. Regardless of anything else, we all deserve empathy, and Amber captures this truth. The stories remain in the mind and in the heart, as do the characters.

Roy Burkhead
- Founder of The Writer's Loft (now known as MTSU's WRITE)
- Founder/editor of *2nd & Church*, a magazine for writers (and others)
- Freelance and trade writer

*W*hen I mentored Amber Hart in MTSU's WRITE program, I was immediately impressed by the characters she created in her writing—characters who came off the page and paraded around in front of me. I heard their voices; I saw their gestures, their mannerisms, and I felt for them as they experienced life's hard knocks. Indeed, they, their communities, and their situations came to life. Many of Amber's characters are down-and-out, and are hoping for a better day tomorrow. In one way or another, these quietly desperate characters find a toe-hold of redemption—from that toe-hold maybe, just maybe, they can survive another day, continue their battle, and come out victorious. Other Amber Hart stories take marvelous flights of the imagination, and transport the reader to strange, yet oddly familiar, places. A couple of the stories are fountainheads for belly laughter. In Amber Hart, the literary world has found a terrifically talented storyteller. I knew from the get-go, I wanted Excalibur Press to be Amber's publisher. So proud, we can count Amber Hart as one of our writers!

Linda Busby Parker
- Mentor, MTSU-WRITE
- Author, *Seven Laurels,* a novel
- Short story and freelance author
- Publisher, Excalibur Press

Some of the stories were originally published in the following journals:

"Teddy's Dead" – *Neon* Issue #41, Summer 2015 and Nominated for Write Well Award 2016

"Our Recovery" – *Storgy*, April 1, 2015

"Happy Birthday, Jasmine" – *Cheat River Review*, Spring 2015

"Thirteen Years" – *Gravel*, May 2015

"Who We Belong To" – *Danforth Review*, Fiction #59 April 13, 2015

"Animal Husbandry" – *LUMINA*, Issue No. 6, May 1, 2016

No Landscape Lasts Forever

Collected Stories

by

Amber Colleen Hart

Excalibur Press 2016

Mobile, Alabama

No Landscape Lasts Forever

Published in the United States of America

by

Excalibur Press

P. O. Box 8797

Mobile, Alabama 36689

Excaliburpress@msn.com

www.excaliburpress.us

Cover Design by Hannah Wilson

www.hbproductions.net

Printed in the United States of America

First Edition, 2016

ISBN 978-0-9820629-4-4

ACKNOWLEDGEMENTS

"If a writer understands his work as something that originates with him but then, with any luck, gets away from him, then what he needs is someone who can grasp the potential of the piece and lead him to that higher ground."

George Saunders

This book is dedicated to all the people who have unfailingly led me to higher ground. I'm certain that without them I would've thrown down my pen, crumpled up all my "shitty first drafts," as Anne Lamott calls them, and pretended this writing thing never happened.

For Karen Alea Ford, former director of WRITE, Middle Tennessee State University's creative writing program, who welcomed me into the writing community and mentored me more than she realizes. Without her, I would not be where I am today.

For my WRITE mentors; Charlotte Rains Dixon, who instilled in me the confidence to share my work, Gloria Ballard, who taught me how to examine my work in ways I carry with me today, and Linda Busby Parker, who encouraged my true voice and showed me through example how to live the writing life with grace and elegance. Together these women created a vortex of learning which shaped me beyond measure. Without them, I would not be the writer I am today.

For my critique group members; Karen Phillips, Wilmoth Foreman, Pam Hanners, who allowed me to veer off from a messy attempt at writing a novel to work on short stories "for a little while." Without their honest critique and wonderful friendship, these stories would not be what they are today.

For my family; my husband Curtis, who has supported me through this process in more ways than I could ever list here. My son Heston, who frequently asked, "You're going to write today, aren't you, Mom?" My daughter Hannah, who left tiny wildflowers next to my computer on days when I needed encouragement most. And, my parents, who have shown me the true meaning of humbleness and unconditional love. Without them, I would not be the person I am today.

And finally, the team at Excalibur Press, who believed in me even on the days I tried to pretend this writing thing never happened.

Amber Colleen Hart

List of Stories

Which Way to Run

I was drunk the day Lorraine got out of prison. I should've gone up there and picked her up. I guarantee she was expecting me. Up to that point, I was always where she told me to be. Eighteen years old and still doing everything my mother told me to do. Even calling her Lorraine instead of Mom. Come here. Go there. Call Roman. Put money in the canteen. Bring candy.

Lorraine and her goddamn candy. Twizzlers, Skittles, Rolos. I forgot the candy once. Once. Jesus, you should've seen her deadeye me that day. A forty-five-minute jail visit full of silence. In the space between mother and daughter, silence means everything and nothing. Everything was wrong and I deserved nothing, least of all her love. That had dried up somewhere between my accident and Roman.

Just to make sure I wouldn't change my mind about going up to the prison, I opened a pint of Roman's Jack Daniels, kicked back half the bottle and listened to the radio. The Jack slowed time. The music smoothed out my panic.

I'd practically had my own prison sentence having to go up there every Thursday for the past eight months. Then having to call Roman after the visits, from a pay phone like Lorraine told me to. The conversation was the same every damn time.

"Yello?" he'd say and wheeze into the phone like the fat ass he was.

"It's Libby."

"Hey, kid."

"Hey."

"How is she? Still okay?"

"The same. Hanging in there."

"She need anything?"

"Just canteen money."

"I figured. It's on its way." Here he'd pause and drag on his cigarette. It was rare for Roman to be without a cigarette hanging from his mouth, bobbing on his every word. "What about you? You need anything, kid?"

"I'm okay," I'd answer and wonder if he even knew my name.

The charade worked. It kept Lorraine quiet, which in turn kept Roman happy enough to pay the rent and give me a little extra to live on. We all played the game.

Through the distance of the phone, I could almost stand Roman. But in person, with his slicked back, greasy hair, and a handful of dirty money, that was a different story. I could feel his obligation. Worse, I could feel my need, strangling me. Together, we were like the shared asshole of conjoined twins.

I drained the pint. By then, Roman and Lorraine would've been standing outside The Huron Valley Women's Correctional Facility. Lorraine in her pale blonde cornrows, tight against her almost albino scalp. Roman sweating and scratching his balls, shrugging. I was done being the candy mule and the carrier pigeon, taking messages back and forth between those two idiots.

Being that I hadn't had a drink in a couple of months, the Jack overpowered me pretty quick. *Here's me turning over a new leaf. Ha.Ha.Ha.* I accidentally lit the filtered end of a cigarette, laughed and waved away the melted plastic smell. I tried again, this time at the right end, and let memories creep in. Blood pulsing out of my wrists, staining my t-shirt and dripping warm onto my bare feet. Lorraine standing frozen in place, glaring at me. Roman yelling at her, "Call 911, goddammit." Me calling out, "Rhonda! Rhonda!" All the Jack Daniels in the world hasn't made that memory go away. And believe me when I say I've tried.

Here's the thing about my memories. They always include Rhonda. Not only had Rhonda and Lo worked together at Galaxy Lanes, they'd been roommates before Lorraine and I moved into our own trailer across the street. Rhonda has pictures of all three of us together in her trailer. It's funny to see me in all those cutesy baby outfits and little bows in my hair. In every one of those pictures Rhonda's holding me tight against her hip and Lorraine looks like she accidentally walked in at the moment the photo was taken. Even though me and Lorraine moved out somewhere around my fourth birthday, I can't remember a time when Rhonda wasn't in my life. Her trailer was my second home. At least until I acted like an asshole and blew up at her. Love in the first degree, I guess.

Rhonda never pulled any bullshit on me. On anyone, for that matter. "You'll find, Libby, that the truth is easier to remember than the lies you make up."

"You gotta keep moving forward, Libby," she'd say. "Make a better life for yourself. Have goals. You're never too young to have goals." Rhonda kept a list of goals tacked up on her refrigerator: Go to cosmetology school. Take business course at Crestwood Community College. Open own salon. Absent from her list was any mention of getting married or having kids. I didn't know yet that some things you couldn't just put on a list to accomplish.

"What about you?" she'd ask me. "What keeps you moving forward?"

At the time, the answer to the question was clear in my mind. I was going to find my father and live happily ever after. Simple as that. I never told Rhonda, though. It felt better to keep my plan to myself. Like a secret between me and my dad, even though he wasn't in on it. So, I'd just shrug and smile.

"Think about it," she'd say. "You have to have goals, Libbs. I'm going to keep asking you until you come up with something." She'd always stare at me a little too long during one of these conversations.

Once in a while, usually after Rhonda riled me up about my future, I'd ask her what she knew about my dad. She must've known I'd find out eventually but she always answered the same. "You gotta ask Lo about him." The problem was I had asked Lorraine about him, a million times, starting all the way back to second grade when that douche bag Joel Watts started teasing me on the bus.

Trailer trash, got no cash. Daddy screwed momma and never came back.

I'd go home and cry to Lo, ask her to tell me about my father. She'd recite the same tight bundle of facts without looking at me. I'd listen, entrenched in the idea of my father, absorb every detail, and add my own until I could no longer distinguish the base lie. I still have a hard time remembering the difference between what Lorraine told me, and what I told myself.

According to Lorraine, my father, "Billy," died in a motorcycle crash before I was born. She didn't use the word hero, that must've been my thought, something implied between the lines. I saw him in my reflection, in the ways I was different from Lorraine. My eyes were his, hazel-gray and almond shaped. Lo's

4

were round, pool-water blue. Where she was wiry and lean, barely five feet, I stood like my father. Tall and thick. Big boned. He would've been one of those men who didn't say much but meant every word he uttered. Known by all, respected and feared for his calculating manner.

God, I used to wish someone — anyone — would ask me about my dad just so I could tell the story, use up my grief and gather their amazement to fill the emptiness inside me. But no one ever asked. In the shadow of my mother no one ever really noticed me.

When Roman came into the picture, Lo stopped telling the story of my father. When I asked, she'd say, "Not now, Libby." At night, when I hit that lonely circle between wanting and not having, I'd work up the courage and pester her again. Eventually she had enough, and she let me know it.

"Jesus Christ, Libby," she said. "Does it matter that I put a roof over your head – every fucking day. Clothe you. Feed you. When's it ever going to be enough? When are you going to let it go?"

Let it go? Without Lorraine's story to bolt me to reality, my fantasies grew to tragic and serious proportions. I envisioned the day Billy learned of me, his joy, the words he'd chosen to respond to the news of me, his gentle kiss on Lorraine's forehead as he asked, "Pregnant? Really?" I saw his last day, the sun setting behind him as he crested the hill on the open road. Then, him skidding on his Harley to avoid a pick-up truck that crossed the dotted line. In my version he lived long enough for Lo to get to the hospital, hold his hand, meet his eyes for the last time as he reached out to touch her belly, then die.

The day I found out the truth about my father, Lorraine lay curled up in bed, clammy and pale. Looking back on it, she probably needed a drink. As in, *needed*. By this time, she was hitting the drink pretty hard.

I rolled out of my bed and padded toward the TV. The trailer was cold. I didn't bother to turn up the heat, though, because the place stayed frigid no matter what. I flipped to Channel 7 to catch a *Mr. Ed* rerun. I liked trying to figure out how they got the horse's mouth to move the way it did. I knew he wasn't talking but I still wondered how they made it look so real.

After *Mr. Ed*, the news popped on. The newscaster pinched off her smile and said, "In traffic, delays continue this morning after a fatal accident involving a motorcyclist and a semi tractor-trailer closed a portion of Highway 20. Witnesses say a motorcyclist struck the semi and then hit a utility pole. The on-ramp is expected to reopen within the next hour." She went back to smiling and announced spotty sunshine throughout the day.

Cool spring air and musty earth smells sifted in under the gap in the front door, mixed with day-old hamburger odor; all the smells circled me. I struggled against the weight of death, stumbled toward the bedroom and crawled into bed with Lorraine.

Lying next to Lorraine I heard phlegm percolate in her throat. She was half in, half out of the covers. One white, stick-leg hung out. Her bleach blonde hair poked out above the sheet.

I squeezed in closer to Lorraine. I shook, swallowed a hundred times, and picked at my eyelashes until they littered my cheeks. Lo pulled herself up, her hair stayed spiked in a rooster comb. The guttural noise moved from her throat to her chest and into a rumbling cough. She spat in the coffee cup on her bedside table, then rubbed her mouth on her sleeve.

"Jesus, Lib. You're up early." She coughed and spat again.

Which Way to Run

I bit down, clenched my teeth. Sweat gathered in the armpits of my pajamas. "Lo?"

"Hmm?"

"I was just wondering ..."

She twisted herself left and right until her back cracked, then lit one of Roman's half-smoked Kools from the ashtray.

"Was my dad... hurt? You know, in the crash?"

Lorraine stubbed out her cigarette in the same cup she'd spit into. She breathed deep, exhaled and headed to the bathroom. The shower squealed on, steam and cigarette smoke fogged up the bedroom. I lay there hoping the contours of silence meant something.

The furnace clinked on. I got out of her bed and stumbled out of the room.

That afternoon I headed straight to Rhonda's after school. She was finishing up a practice haircut on one of those creepy mannequin heads with no eyes.

"Hey, Libby," Rhonda shot me a quick smile then went back to studying the head in front of her. She squinted and tilted her own head this way and that way then set her scissors down. "My work here is done." She took a small bow.

Rhonda tied her apron tighter against her trim waist and smoothed her skin-tight pants against her butt. She emptied a Goody's powder into her Ginger Ale, stirred, and sipped through a straw.

"What's wrong, Libbs?" Rhonda asked, teasing up her hair in the mirror. She brushed hair off the chair and motioned for me to sit. Sometimes we talked like this, me in the chair talking to the Rhonda I saw in the mirror.

"Lo told me about my dad," I blurted out. Excitement burned down my throat and into my empty stomach. My face went prickly, then my cheeks, my chest.

Rhonda's shoulders slackened and her face sagged into her age. She gave me a look like a dog that's just been kicked. "Oh, honey. I'm sorry."

She pulled her arms away and crossed them over her chest. "How much did she tell you?"

"All of it." I hadn't planned on lying. But when you have all day to think about things, sometimes your plans change. I looked away from the Rhonda in the mirror. My mind trailed back and forth filling in blanks, jotting down notes, points where I could come across convincing if I needed to.

"Lord," Rhonda sighed. "I told her that lie would come back to haunt her." She came around the chair and faced me. "And, here we are," she said. "All things considered, it's probably better that none of us knows who your dad is. Judging from the company your mom keeps, he can't be anything too special."

"Lo doesn't even know who he is?"

Rhonda tucked my hair behind my ears. Her face hardened in a way I hadn't seen before. "Listen, honey. Your mom had some dark days before you came along. The things she went through. Well … there's a certain kind of darkness that gets right inside a person and doesn't ever leave, no matter how hard they try."

I didn't bother to ask Rhonda just exactly how Lo might be *trying real hard*. Rhonda blabbered on about Lorraine not being a bad person and that I should remember she was doing the best she could. Rhonda was wasting her breath. I already knew what a stellar mother Lorraine was. After all, she'd put a trailer roof over my head, clothed me in ninety-nine cent Goodwill specials, and made sure I had Wonder Bread to eat.

Which Way to Run

Before Lorraine went to prison, it didn't take a genius to figure out things were getting hot and heavy between those two, especially with Roman's Mercedes parked on the lawn next to our gravel driveway each morning. The late night laughing and beer tab hissing and bed bumping made it pretty obvious. I was happy for Lorraine. Someone loved her and not because she was the nearest piece of ass bringing drinks on demand. At least, not at first.

I spent a lot of time at Rhonda's. I'd flip through the TV channels while she talked her way through her latest cosmetology assignment. It was great until Rhonda started to ask a lot of questions. First, of course, she wanted to know what goals I'd come up with. But then she started asking a bunch of other shit.

"Did Roman spend the night? Again? I tell you; this boyfriend of your mom's is no good. What kind of a man drives a Mercedes Benz? In a trailer park?"

Rhonda didn't wait for me to answer.

"I'll tell you what kind. A drug dealer, that's who." Rhonda took her Goody's powder out and stirred it into her drink, shaking her head as she stared out the window. "Just because folks live in a trailer park does not mean they have to be trash. Or hang around trash."

Trailer Trash, Got No Cash.

She went on like that, moving shit around her makeshift salon and eyeing the Mercedes like it had a heartbeat of its own.

"If your mama's not careful she's gonna get strung out on drugs. Lord God, she'll be even more useless to you if that happens."

Even more useless?

Like I said, Rhonda didn't pull any punches so I should've been cool with what she said but to hear the truth spoken so matter-of-factly sucked the air right out of the room. It's one thing to talk shit about your family and quite another when someone else does it.

"You're the one who moved us into this piece of shit trailer park in the first place, Rhonda. If anybody's useless around here it's you. Useless and full of shit!"

I'm not proud of the things I said. Especially the part I threw in about her being a two-bit cocktail waitress who'd never amount to anything. And though I've tried to block it out of my memory, I know I spat on the floor of her trailer before I hightailed it out of there.

Rhonda chased after me, said she was sorry. Hard to believe, her apologizing to me. I should've just turned around and heard her out, but instead I yelled, "Leave me the fuck alone," and kept right on running.

A few days later Rhonda left a letter in the mailbox. In it she said she was sorry she upset me and that she was worried about me. She mentioned not liking Roman's influence on Lo, like he was the Big Bad Wolf amid the oh-so-innocent. But in my opinion, Little Red Riding Hood had problems way before the Big Bad Wolf showed up. Red's mother let her walk through the wolf-infested woods for Christ's sake. Something was wrong there.

Rhonda ended the letter with, "If you need me, you know where to find me."

Yeah, yeah. I threw the letter in the trash. But within an hour I pulled it back out and stuck it in my sock drawer.

The thing is, I *had* noticed certain things about my home life before Rhonda brought it up. Roman's dirty socks balled up on

10

the floor and his cigarettes overflowing in every ashtray. Mud got dragged in on the bottom of his shoes, dropped on the linoleum and gathered in the corners. Even on the days Roman didn't come over, he was there with us in the dirt.

Then this thing happened that sort of pushed me closer to the edge. Lorraine didn't go to work. I hadn't even thought about her being home because she never missed work. When she opened her bedroom door and trudged into the living room I nearly choked on my cheese curls.

I looked her over, checking to see what kind of sick she was. Her blue eyes were empty, like staring straight into a hole. She was hollowed out. Gunk had started to gather at her gum line like clotted wet bread. Her skin was an odd color.

"You sick?"

"What do you think?" She hissed and shuffled past me. She wandered into the kitchen and banged dishes around. "This place is a goddamn disaster," she said, like it was my fault.

Let me point out Lorraine was never a very good housekeeper, but every once in a while she'd decide to clean up the place. She'd boost up the volume on WKFM country radio and we'd spend half a Saturday working our way from one end of the trailer to the other armed with Windex and bleach. When the place was cleaned up you couldn't really tell most of our stuff was hand-me-downs. I wouldn't have minded if someone dropped by unexpectedly.

But, like I said, I'd noticed a few things. One of them was, that kind of cleaning hadn't happened in a long time. Roman noticed too. He'd say things like, "How can you live like this?" or "Would it kill you to straighten this place up?" Sometimes he'd just shake his greasy head and say, "Jesus H. Christ, Lorraine."

At first the mess didn't bother me. In the mornings I'd look outside to see if the Mercedes was there. If it wasn't, I'd settle in on the couch in front of the TV, unwrap a candy bar, pop open a can of Coke, and veg out. After a month of those kinds of Saturdays, though, I'd had enough. The place got pretty rank, a mix between rotten trash and body odor, and I couldn't take it anymore. I got out the cleaning supplies, cranked up the radio, and started emptying out the ashtrays.

Lorraine yelled to me from the bedroom, "Turn that goddamn radio down!"

I turned it off and went to the closed door of her bedroom. "I'm cleaning."

She mumbled something I couldn't make out, but got the gist of. I tried to open the door but it was locked. That made no sense, locking a paper-thin door with a one-inch gap at the bottom of it.

"What?" I asked.

"Do it without the fucking radio on."

"Okay," I said and stared at the door. "Do you need anything in there?"

After a minute she said, "Cigarettes."

I ran down to Jimmy's 7-11, bought two packs of Kools and jogged back home. Even though I was underage, Jimmy didn't hesitate. He knew they were for Lorraine. Everybody knew about my mom in some way or another. It was rare for me to meet someone who didn't immediately ask, "Are you Lorraine's kid?" It got harder and harder for me to answer without almost asking, "Yeah, are you my dad, by chance?" I never had the courage to ask out loud. Mostly because the men who were doing the asking were the men I didn't want saying yes.

Back at the trailer I rapped on her bedroom door with one knuckle, and slid the Kools under the gap of the door. Within seconds the acrid mix of nicotine and tar tinged my nose. It was like throwing raw steak at a caged tiger.

Once I started cleaning, I couldn't stop. I noticed things I never had before; how the chairs didn't really fit around the kitchen table, the way none of the dishes matched, the random piles of paper cluttering up the trailer. The chaos made me worry. That very day I started a written list of items in my room and their placement. *Red spiral notebook on right side of desktop, one inch from right edge. Blue Bic pen capped, centered parallel to notebook. Six pennies flush with top left of desk, head side up, starting from left 1972, 1990, 1991, 1993, 1994, 1997. Cassettes alphabetized by first letter of first song on side B.* I planned on checking the list as soon as I got home from school each day, then I'd rearrange the items and chronicle them for the next day. The list got pretty extensive and ate up my time, but it made me feel better. At least this was something I controlled.

Taking care of myself, making sure Lorraine was still alive, avoiding Roman and the kids at school; it was more work than you'd imagine. By the time I hit tenth grade, I was primed in managing disaster.

***

The accident wasn't really an accident. Not that I meant to do it, I just got carried away. My impulse control was at an all-time low. After I counted the items on my list and made sure nothing was out of order, I had these thoughts—camera shots really—pop into my mind.

Click. Lo white and stiff in her bed. Click. Lo's blue eyes clouded over and dull. Click. Me covered in blood standing over her. Each click brought me enormous relief.

The first time it happened, I was at Jimmy's. One minute I'm looking at a bag of barbeque potato chips, the next I'm seeing myself holding a kitchen knife, standing at Lo's bedside with blood puddled beneath my bare feet. The thing that disturbed me most was knowing I'd be the one to have to clean it up.

Jimmy must've thought I lost my mind, standing there blinking slow, mouth half-open. "Cat got your tongue today, Libby?"

His forced laugh jarred me back to the shit surrounding me, chips and gum and liquor bottles, rubbers and rolling papers and cigarettes. The camera clicks stopped. I cleared my throat and shrugged. I felt like I'd just finished running a marathon. It took all my energy just to hand Jimmy the money.

"You alright?" Jimmy pushed two packs of Kools toward me on the counter.

Oh sure, Jimmy. I'm good. I may or may not have just killed my mother. That's all. I nodded like a retard and left.

Those snapshots came in flashes more and more often, unexpected. It started as just one click of a whole scene then worked its way up to around twenty clicks. Close-ups of the knife or Lo's dead white face, her mouth frozen in surprise, the sadness trapped in her eyes, or the revenge in mine. I didn't feel bad. I didn't feel anything.

On my bed the day of the accident, the reel started rolling but didn't provide the usual relief. Pretend killing Lorraine wasn't enough anymore. I focused on Roman, and hoped to see images of him but I guess I didn't care enough about him to kill him. I went to the kitchen and cleaned. Bleached the counter tops. Chipped away at the crud baked on the stove.

When I reorganized the silverware drawer, I found a fork with crusted egg on it. I washed the silverware by hand. All of it.

14

Which Way to Run

When I got to the sharp knives I slowed down so as not to cut myself. I saved the big knife with the cracked handle for last, ran my hand over the dull side of the blade under the water beneath the bubbles.

The problem with knives, silverware in general, is they really need a good hard scrubbing to get the germs off. Isn't it odd to stick sharp things, like a fork, in your mouth? It's like we take our lives in our hands every day by jamming four sharp prongs into our heads. It's amazing how much trust we put in ourselves and others to stay alive.

Anybody could decide to run their car over the median full speed and crash into another car, or swallow a few dozen pills, or turn the gas on in the trailer. Wouldn't take long.

I was contemplating the impressive reality of all of this when I felt the burn of soap under my skin. Blood gathered in a cluster and sat blobbed on top of a fresh cut as if it were making a decision what to do next, which way to run. I put the tip of the knife on the wound and the blood grabbed on, disappearing into a watery smear. I cut a little deeper and watched the blob grow bigger. I slipped the knife crosswise over that cut and waited to see what would happen.

No matter how many times I cut, the blood just seeped out and sat there, undecided. I rinsed my fingers under the sting of cold water. And that's when I caught sight of a thick blue vein on my wrist. Decisive, pulsing blood. I sliced into the long Y shaped vein. Blood oozed out like hot caramel across ice cream. I went deeper, wondering if the blood would follow the same path or forge a new one. I plunged the knife in and dragged it up my forearm. Blood jumped up the knife without hesitation then raced back down the blade.

I'd never felt pain like that before. But, no matter how far I stabbed the knife into my skin, or how many times I sliced, I just stayed floating outside myself watching intently, mesmerized.

***

My memory from then is spotty. Roman picked me up, wrapped my wrist in a stained kitchen towel, then yelled at Lorraine to get her goddamn head on straight and dial 911. I remember thinking he was probably worried about me bleeding all over his Mercedes on the drive to the emergency room. When I came to after getting stitched up, I realized it might've been more serious than him not wanting me to ruin his seats.

Jeopardy was on. Except for the condescending voice of Alex Trebek, I was alone in a half-cocked hospital bed. The nurse came in and said, "You're awake." I answered her Jeopardy style, "What is ... the point?" She handed me two pills in a tiny paper cup. I didn't bother to ask what they were before I swallowed them down.

I woke up a little while later when Roman cleared his throat.

"Hey, kid."

I didn't say anything to him right away. My stitched wrist pulsed in unison with the thought, *fuck you, fuck you, fuck you.* Blood travelled through my bandaged hand, swelled and bunched up in my fingertips.

"Where's my mom?"

Roman hesitated, shifted under the weight of his fat ass. "She's getting her head together. You gave her a pretty good scare."

I peered down at my hand. Guilt settled on my chest. If it weren't for Roman, I might not be alive. If he had been sitting

16

closer, I might've thanked him or called him a rat bastard. The spiral in my head started. If it weren't for Roman, Lorraine would still be my fucking mother, sad as she was in that role, but she would be mine. My fun loving, alcoholic mother who cleaned up the goddamn trash in her trailer once in a while. Bringing that shit around her, weak as she was, Roman knew what he was doing. And now he'd ruined her, ruined my sad, beautiful mom. Maybe I'd still get something from her if it weren't for Roman. Or I could be dead. Either way, Roman was responsible for my life. Rat Bastard. Should've just let me die, instead of killing Lorraine the way he was.

"Your mom … she just got carried away a little. She's getting cleaned up. Right now. She'll be good as new when you get home."

A new mom. I could hardly wait to see that. The thump-thump in my hand had relocated to my head.

"She loves you, kid. You might try keeping that in mind. It ain't been easy for her."

I laughed out loud and pressed the button for the nurse about fifty times. She came in with a put-out look on her face. "I'm going to be sick," I said. I was sweating like I had typhoid fever and must've looked like it too because she told Roman he'd have to go.

I saw spots behind my eyes and couldn't catch my breath. Why is it so hard to stop crying once you start? I felt like an asshole, blubbering like that in front of the nurse. She left the room and came back about ten seconds later with a couple small blue pills and a Styrofoam cup with a straw. I took the pills and crashed before I could even dry my face.

Half a dozen morons at the hospital had to come by and ask me the same questions over and over again before I could be released. Doctors, nurses, a social worker. In the end they sent me home with some more of those blue pills. The nurse told me to take one a day to help with my feelings. She said it was normal to feel depressed after an "episode" such as mine.

Roman drove me home. I walked in the front door and found Lorraine on the couch wrapped in her robe. She stood up and came toward me, her hair washed, the gunk from her teeth gone. She fixed her eyes on me in a dead stare. I didn't realize how much behind the scenes fantasizing I'd done about this moment until she opened her mouth.

"You pull that shit again and you'll be out on your ass before you can say *boo*. Do I make myself clear?"

I would've settled for a flicker of worry or relief to show in her face, a stroke of love. Instead, her beady eyes bearing down on me let me know right then I'd fucked up her life from the minute I was born. A little something she hadn't bargained for.

"Yes. Clear," I said. I pulled my bag of pills off the counter and went to my room. Welcome Home.

The murmuring in the living room went on for a while. Voices rose and fell. I lay down on my bed, settled into the knowledge Lo had just imparted to me and began to hate myself to the same degree she hated me. The small collection of things I owned surrounded me, reminding me how my needs must've set Lorraine back, made her resent me even more. I vowed not to eat her food or use her toilet paper, breathe her air. I'd make myself small. Invisible. Insignificant. I'd show her.

I took two little blue pills out, drank them down without water. I'd be damned if I was going into the kitchen for a glass of water. I fell asleep to the drum of Randy Travis' *I Told You So* seeping in from the living room.

18

Which Way to Run

Three pills a day kept me flying high, kept me from feeling anything including hunger. It helped me get through GED classes. I didn't make friends, didn't talk to anyone. Made my life easier.

Would've been nice to see Rhonda. I'd had a dream about Rhonda while I was in the hospital. She was beside my bed, crying and saying my name over and over, telling me she loved me. I wanted to reach out to hug her but I felt like someone had sewn me into the bed and tied weights around my neck. In my dream, I was trying to tell Rhonda how sorry I was, that I *would* figure out my future. I even screamed for help, but my tongue was trapped under the spell of morphine. I couldn't even cry. She patted my arm, wiped her face and left. When I woke up, the room had gone black with night and reeked of Lysol.

My life went like this: go to class, come home, go to my room, fall asleep. Get up the next morning and do the same things all over again. Sometimes I'd watch the news, laugh at the shit considered worthy enough to be broadcast; suicide bombers, murders, robberies, traffic jams, and thunderstorms. Hilarious, really. Who cares what travesties we can foist upon one another. Just think of what we can do to ourselves. That shit never makes the news.

On the days Lo had to work, Roman came by and picked her up and left behind the lingering scent of cigars and cologne. They might as well have been married with all their predictability. Consistency is sometimes scarier than unpredictability. They reminded me of Lucy and Ricky on *I Love Lucy*. Only Lucy never sold drugs for Ricky at a bowling alley and ended up face down in lane seven with a cop's knee in her back and a billy club across her shoulders.

Hey, Lorraine, I didn't show up because I'm pretty much done with you. What's that, you say? You don't care? Exactly my point.

Goddammit if Rhonda wasn't right, telling the truth *was* easier than lying. The consequences would probably run about the same, too. I got up from the table expecting to feel drunk, but actually felt pretty solid on my feet. I found a working pen in the junk drawer—a miracle in and of itself—and a scrap piece of paper large enough to jot a few notes on. I emptied the ashtray, threw away the bottle of Jack, wiped down the table with my sleeve, and started.

1. *Get a job*
2. *Call Rhonda*

Banksy Blues

I lie wedged in the crack of the couch, a throw piled up on top of me, and listen to the news. A newborn baby has been found in a nearby apartment dumpster. A tenant made the discovery when he heaved his trash into the bin. A dead infant thrown in with other people's trash.

"Who would do such a thing? To a newborn, no less," my step-mom chides from the kitchen. "She could've given that baby to anyone. So many women without children, and she goes and does that." Maureen tsk-tsks with the same force she uses when I forget to empty the dishwasher. "Seriously, Abigail? How can you *forget?*" She chatters so much that I hardly hear her anymore.

I want to scream at Maureen, at the TV, at the constant influx of baby news that hits me from all sides and prods me to confess to the situation I'm in. Own up. I practice all the time in my head and have practically blurted it out a dozen times or more. *I'm pregnant. I'm pregnant. I'm pregnant.* The words become a mantra, a meditative chant, nothing more than a series of sounds strung together to dull the mind. My stomach pushes up and flutters from hunger or from nausea. It's too soon to tell.

The weight of my unborn baby pulls me down further into the couch. I sink lower into the depths of the situation. *We* sink, together. Inseparable. If the couch could just finish the job and suck me down into oblivion, all of my problems would be solved. I wouldn't even have to take final exams.

"Abigail Marie." Maureen is over me, preventing my disappearance. "How many times have I told you not to bury yourself under these cushions? You are going to ruin this couch." She punches up the cushions with each word. "Go do something with yourself—besides lie around." Then she starts in on how when she was sixteen she wouldn't have been caught dead at home. I can't picture Maureen at sixteen. I can't picture her doing anything other than lighting one of her long Chesterfield's, painting her nails, sighing into her coffee cup.

I stand up, not because Maureen has told me to, but because I know what my stomach has decided. Sweat warms my armpits, saliva gathers in my mouth, the back of my throat opens up all the way to my stomach. The alien pod presses against my insides, and I have to quickstep to the bathroom. Maureen says something but I can't hear her over the train inside my head. This kind of vomit is hard to hold back. I crank on the shower and hope the water beating into the tub will cover up the noise of me heaving.

Maureen is the only woman to set foot in our house since my mother left us. I haven't seen or heard from my mother since she disappeared, six years ago not counting the day she broke in and stole the television. I wouldn't exactly call it a break-in as my father never changed the locks. I guess he had the same hope I did back then. He never said. At least she gave him the courtesy of saying "good-bye," even if it included a few other choice words and phrases. I would've settled for a hug or some other small gesture but I was never part of her equation.

God, how they argued. She screamed and cried, and threw anything she could get her hands on. My father yelled at her to calm down—which only made her worse—and dodged the objects she hurled his way. They played out this scene the night she left for good. But instead of my mother collapsing on the floor in a heap of tears like she usually did, she stopped crying altogether and quietly announced she'd had enough. From my bedroom I heard my father exhale and plop down heavily into his recliner.

"So, that's it? You're just going to walk out?"

"I told you from the beginning," she said, "I am just not cut out for this."

"For what exactly, Cassandra?"

"For *this*. For being someone's wife. Someone's mother! I can't pretend to be someone I'm not, Phil. You act like me giving birth should've somehow activated my motherly instincts. Like it was going to be that simple."

My father didn't argue the point.

The worst part about her leaving was the silence that followed. Inside the silence, I invented apologies and tenderness and an epic return of my mother that never came. Inside the silence, I began to understand how things worked and didn't work. A thick silence took up residence in place of my mother and spread out in the space between my father and me.

About a year after my mother left, I came home from school to find a willowy woman standing in the living room smoothing down her frosted hair with her Lee Press-On nails, and smiling too much. I didn't know who she was but I knew why she was there. My father sat perched on the edge of his Lazyboy with a blank face.

"This is Maureen," he said, as if her name explained everything I needed to know. The whole scene seemed like an awkwardly staged play in which I had no lines. A few weeks later, a U-Haul backed up to our front door and unpacked about a hundred boxes full of Maureen's junk, her mismatched furniture, and a half-dead cat named Mr. Murray. Team Maureen and Murray crowded out the last hints of my mother. I swallowed down a new kind of loneliness, a self-contained sadness that belonged only to me.

In the first year, I made myself small and listened for clues to our future.

I constantly wondered how long it would take before Maureen told my father she didn't want to be my stand-in mother. How long before that U-Haul came back and emptied out the house. Emptied out my father. I searched for signs of waning interest. I listened for angry words, or crying jags, or disdainful glances. Instead, Maureen filled the house with stewed meals, brightly painted furniture—repurposed, as she called it—rose-scented air freshener, the constant snap of gum and tap of fingernails, all of which gave me a massive headache.

Now the only time I get a headache is when I come really close to telling Maureen and my father about the baby. What if, for all Maureen's loyalty, me having a baby ends up being *the* thing that sends her packing? "A grandmother? At my age! No thank you." I can't put my father through that kind of abandonment again. Not after six years. I have to be sure I break the news in a way that will prevent ruining my father's happiness. The weight of time is pushing me.

What I need to do is find out if the at-home test I did was right. Who knows, I could've messed it up. Besides, how accurate could a pregnancy test from the Dollar Zone be anyway?

On Monday after my algebra exam, I head to the health department on North Rd. Because I have Job Corps for sixth hour, I can ditch school without the hassle of being caught. Job Corps means going out into the "real world"—as Maureen calls it—and earning a living at the local fast food hole. Burger King will have to live without my French frying expertise for one day.

The lobby is as big as the gymnasium at school, but with buffed white tiles that make my tennis shoes squeak every time I take a step. A pale skinny lady with thin lips sits at the check-in window. Her nametag reads, "Denise." She doesn't bother to look up when I get to the window, just keeps typing.

"Can I help you?"

"I...um..."

"Do you have an appointment?"

"No." I squeeze the strap on my backpack with both hands like I'm dangling from a rope. I'm sweating and my stomach gets busy curdling the Twix bar I ate for lunch.

"I...um...I think...it's possible I might be..." I lean in close so my mouth is inside the window. "Pregnant?" My face burns all the way down to my neck.

Denise finally lifts her head and glares at me as if I'm the dumbest person she's run across today.

"You don't need an appointment for a pregnancy test."

"I didn't know."

"Name?"

"Abigail."

"Full name."

"Abigail ... Hinks."

"Have a seat. The nurse will call you back shortly."

I haven't even stepped away from the window before Denise yells, "Next!"

I find a chair nearest the entrance. That's it? No paperwork to fill out? No explaining? I should've given a fake name. An old lady limps in and the automatic door stands open behind her like an invitation. I'm up, squeaking toward the door, when I hear my name yelled.

"Abigail."

Shit. I'm frozen between the opposing open doors. Invitations to two entirely different parties.

"Abigail."

I turn, expecting to find Denise staring a hole into my head, but she's busy with the old lady who's just now made it to the window.

A nurse leads me to the back. I pee on a stick in the bathroom and leave it by the sink as instructed, then go find room #3 and wait.

Sitting on the counter next to the sink is a life-sized plastic womb with a baby inside of it, curled upside down in a giant O. It's the same sort of hard, plastic model as the ones in biology lab that look like someone chopped a person in half then colored them with the lightest crayons they could find. Totally fake. I feel the baby flutter inside of me, twisting and turning maybe. Bunching up and making me feel like I need to pee again.

The nurse comes in. She steals sideways glances at me as she slides the other chair up in front of me, clipboard in hand. Her face is pinched up, stern.

"Well. You are definitely pregnant." It's the first time the words have been spoken aloud. She studies my face. "I'd say right around twelve to fourteen weeks. We'll know for sure after an exam."

I fumble with my backpack and say, "Today? I need to get home."

"You'll need to make an appointment for the exam. Let me get you a packet first. It goes over the prenatal appointment schedule. You've already missed the first trimester so it's really important you come back for an exam and follow up appointments. Plus, you need to watch your diet and get on some prenatal vitamins as soon as possible."

The next thing I know I'm bent over the trashcan, throwing up Twix on top of used rubber gloves and needle wrappers. All I can think about is how I want out of this place right now, away from the plastic uterus in faded red, white and cream hues, and away from the thumping of my heartbeat over the baby's.

The nurse stands and says, "The throwing up will get better as you move into your second trimester." She leaves the room then comes back with a handful of pamphlets and Xeroxed papers. "Make sure you come back, okay?"

I sit in Potter Park on a swing, not moving, and wonder if the father of my unborn child is dead. He has to be. At first I tell myself he's back in juvie, that's the reason I haven't seen him around. Probably got caught tagging the overpass again. But it's been three weeks since I've seen him. He'd be out by now unless he's committed a more serious crime than vandalism. I've scanned the police blotters, searched for his real name. Gordon Sleight. Nothing. Still, I haven't seen any new graffiti. At least not with his tag name "SL8" on it.

I wait on the swing in hopes he'll come by, plop down on a nearby picnic table and give me his lecture about how graffiti is art in the truest sense of the word.

"Just ask Banksy," he'd say as he smoothed back his out-of-control hair for the hundredth time. The first time he mentioned the street artist, I didn't know much. "You *do* know who Banksy is, don't you?" SL8 asked.

I nodded, repeated what I'd heard about the famous graffiti artist. "He's the guy who tags buildings without anyone ever

29

seeing him do it?" I couldn't help how my voice curled into a question.

"He paints amazing shit. And, yeah, he strikes and runs. Most people don't even know what he looks like."

SL8 paced and ate his way through one of the candy bars he'd lifted from the 7-11. In between bites, he ranted about the difference between vandalism and art and how the police wouldn't know real art if it bit them on the ass. Then he said, "They may be able to paint over my art but they can't stop the Banksy Effect."

"The what?"

"The Banksy Effect." He said it right in my face, piercing me with his glare. "Because of Banksy, people are starting to believe in graffiti. Accept it as real art. They're even paying shitloads of money for it." He translated this to him becoming famous one day. "But not here. Not in Poughkeepsie. I need to get to NYC. Tag the whole city with my signature 8. You'll see it one day and you'll know it's me. You'll say, 'I knew that dude.'" By then he was staring out past me into his future.

I've never met anyone like SL8 before. He actually thinks about things: art, injustice, being someone. His artwork is detailed, meaningful. *Anti-establishment.* SL8's father has already told him he has to go to college and has to study pre-law.

"He's got another thing coming if he thinks I'm going to follow in his bourgeoisie footsteps."

I always nod in agreement when SL8 starts one of his rants, but part of me wonders what's so bad about driving a nice car and having money. If it weren't for his father's bourgeoisie lifestyle, we'd have to find some other place to be alone.

The only thing I have to offer to match SL8's brilliance is sex, which he accepts without hesitation. Even when I fumble around,

Banksy Blues

not knowing what to do, he holds my face in his hands and says, "It's okay, babe." I glom onto him like a life raft in a sea squall. It's all well and good until the raft takes on an extra body, unborn as it is. Maybe I shouldn't have told him about the baby.

I check my watch. My shift at Burger King is ending now so it's safe to head home. Safe as long as I don't mess up the cushions or sass Maureen or, heaven forbid, forget to empty the dishwasher. Safe as long as I keep the baby hidden.

For the next week, I avoid the health department. On my way home, I loop around the street and go past the 7-11 instead. On Friday my head hurts and I'm so tired I squat on the curb to gather enough strength to go on. That's when I see something painted on the side of the Ready-Cash building.

A huge neon red question mark with arcing curves and sharp corners glows, pulses. Below the question mark a shadowy, indistinct figure holds giant scissors in one hand and a string in the other. The string has been snipped mid-way. At the other end of the dangling string is a balloon with a tiny child tucked inside, floating toward a dark cloud. Inside the scissors, I see the tag: SL8.

I run home, my feet on fire from pounding on the pavement. At my front door I hesitate, breathe in and out until the burning in my lungs passes. Then stand there, crying and spitting, my arms in a half hug around my middle when the door chirks open.

"Well, are you going to come in or just stand there all day?" Maureen asks. Then, "Oh my God, Abby. What's wrong, honey? What's the matter?" She wraps her arms around me and pulls me into the house. And, I can't help it, I sob into her arms and tell her everything. I tell her about Gordon's artwork on the side of the building, and how he's the same as Banksy and my mother—how they all strike and run, strike and run. By the time I get through

31

telling her about the baby, Maureen is squeezing me so tight I can barely breathe.

"Oh my God, Abby. Twelve weeks. Why didn't you say something sooner?"

"I was going to but it just never seemed like the right time. And I thought you'd get mad and leave and it would be all my fault."

"Leave? Is that what you think? I'd just pack up and leave after all this time?"

"It happens. It keeps happening."

"Not with me it hasn't. I had to convince your father of the same thing—it never occurred to me to include you in the conversation. Look, honey, I may not know who this Banksy character is you're rambling on about," she says, "but, I was sixteen once, Abigail. Believe it or not. And I know a little more about this kind of thing than you think."

Maureen squeezes me again. "We'll figure out what to tell your father. He's ... well ... he'll come around. Don't you worry." As she smoothes down my hair, one of her Lee Press-Ons gets stuck. She untangles her hand, rips off the fake nail and throws it onto the coffee table. "These damn things are more trouble than they're worth." Mr. Murray swishes by, rubs against my leg like we've been friends forever. "Stupid cat," Maureen says, shoos him away with her foot, and pulls me in closer.

Animal Husbandry

The first time I showed up to Sunday dinner with Pat, my father didn't even bother to look up from his latest copy of *The American Journal of Medicine*. He feigned interest in the cover story, "Recurrent Pancreatitis, Rash and Diarrhea: A complex combination." But I knew better. I was going through a bit of a varmint phase and my father did not approve. He stirred his Bombay and tonic and pretended not to be disgusted over my date being a raccoon. Mom smiled and backed her way toward the kitchen, the panic in her eyes directed at me. I fixed Pat a drink and excused myself to the kitchen where my mother stood piling steaming meatballs into a Ziploc bag.

"You should've told me he was a raccoon, Janey," she said.

"What difference does it make, Mom?"

"I would've made something different. Pasta, maybe. I made meatballs!"

"Pat likes meatballs."

"He's not vegetarian? Like...the others?"

"No, Mom. Pat's an omnivore. The others were herbivores."

"Well, you still should've prepared your father and me."

We made it through dinner thanks to my mother's well-trained hospitality and my father's reserve bottle of Bombay gin. For a few weeks afterward, I fooled myself into believing they were beginning to accept my alternative lifestyle. But the next time I saw them, I got a different impression. I'd no more than poured myself a cup of coffee when my father started in on a rant about vermin. He called them filthy and promiscuous. Disease spreading rodents.

"You're making assumptions based on social misperceptions," I said.

"I'm not making assumptions, Janey. I'm a doctor. I've seen it."

"You're being narrow-minded."

"And you're taking unnecessary risks with your health."

"But, I'm in love."

My father shook his head. My mother wrung out her dishrag and wiped the same spot on the table repeatedly.

"You have to understand, Janey. Your father and I grew up in a different time. People who dated outside their genus were considered..."

"Trashy," my father said, "and that's putting it nicely."

"But I'm in love. Doesn't that count for something?"

"It'll pass," my father said.

"Oh, like love is a thing that just passes, Dad."

"Of course not, dear," my mother said. "What your father means is that it would be easier for you if you found someone, you know, normal."

"You mean someone with two arms and two legs. Because that defines what normal is, right? And by the way, raccoons are rodents."

The air got a little stuffy for a while. Mom brought out a lemon icebox cake and busied herself with cutting it into precisely measured slices, while my father clicked through the television channels about a hundred times. I slipped some Bailey's into my

Animal Husbandry

coffee to keep from asking them what they could possibly know about love.

Pat and I split up less than a year later. I came home early from work and caught him dumpster diving with my neighbor. The break-up took its toll on me. I didn't leave my apartment except to go to work. Couldn't eat or sleep with any consistency. Wouldn't answer my phone. When I finally showed up to Sunday dinner at my parents', the first thing my father asked was, "Where's Pat?"

"We broke up," I said quietly.

My mother sucked in a breath and sighed, "Thank God."

I braced myself for the *I told you so* that was sure to come.

"Honestly, Janey, he smelled terrible," Mom said.

"Downright putrid," my father added.

"Why didn't either of you say anything?"

"You wouldn't have listened," my father said. "You seem hell bent on dating strays."

Sometimes the truth is quite a low blow.

When I met Pat, I did notice a certain odor about him. But, I thought he was a true outdoorsman, and as such tended to smell like dried leaves and old pennies. Tangy. Edgy. And, it turned out, homeless. As soon as I figured out he was living on the streets, I moved him in with me. I cooked his meals, taught him how to grocery shop, bought him scented body soap and heavy-duty nail clippers. I didn't realize he had a lifestyle of his own.

No doubt my parents were overemphasizing the extent of Pat's stench as a way to restate their displeasure with me dating a rodent. However, a month or so after I kicked Pat out, I ran into him outside my apartment and realized there was more to it than that. I watched as he backed out of my neighbor's trashcan, ass first, completely unaware of me. Deciding to be the bigger person, I squelched the urge to chuck one of my tennis shoes at him.

"Hey, Pat." I tried to sound nonchalant.

He started scrambling, bicycling his legs down the trashcan like I was Annie Oakley pointing a shotgun at his thieving ass. When he saw me, he let out a little sigh. When he squinted at me, his eyes disappeared into the black of his mask.

A heavy pause hung between us.

"So, how's slut face?" I nodded to the next building over.

Pat sighed again and pinched the space between his eyes, a thing I'd seen my father do at least a thousand times during my childhood. He started hedging, staring at me out of the corner of his eye as if to say, *Shit happens, Janey* and *You can't help who you fall in love with.* But I couldn't focus over the sharp smell hitting the back of my throat. A mix of odors, like canned cat food and rotten hardboiled eggs.

Pat stood there shifting from one scrawny foot to the other like he always did when he was uncomfortable. God, was he ugly. His nose, peeling from rooting around in the garbage all the time to feed his filthy habit. His fingernails, packed with the remnants of half eaten meals and dirty diapers. That ridiculous mask he refused to take off. And this guy had been the love of my life?

"Well, I gotta go, Pat," I said.

Hell bent on strays or not, my parents should've said something to me. Spared me the embarrassment of my misjudgment early on.

I didn't date for a while after Pat. My best friend Margo made me sign an official contract with her saying I promised never to date a raccoon again. We were drunk, both of us crying into our margaritas over the assholes we'd been duped by. I thought we

Animal Husbandry

were long past the point of her trying to talk me into dating normal guys, and me pushing her into trying something different. Just two drunk girls at the bar slurring over our losses, but then Margo asked, "Didn't his mask bother you?"

"Why would his mask bother me? He's a raccoon, Margo. They all wear masks."

"I don't know… because it seems like… it would feel like… a masked rapist or something."

"Beats the hell out of lights-out, missionary-style, every-Tuesday-Thursday-and-Saturday-sex, doesn't it?"

Margo blushed and stirred her margarita. I knew right then what type of sex she was accustomed to. I also knew she wasn't as hip to my alternative lifestyle as I thought she'd been.

Margo didn't understand. My parents didn't approve. Pat was gone and I had a trail of shitty relationships behind me. All of this left me pretty damn lonely. I suppose that's why I ended up going home with a mole. He sent me a drink. We talked for a while. Margo tried to persuade me to say no but something about him not having eyes intrigued me. Not having to hold his gaze or worry about what my hair looked like, felt like a relief. One less facade to put up with.

Back at my place, he touched me gently here and there, gathering information through his senses. I felt wildly uninhibited. Close to him and yet so far away. Like an observer thrown into the ring. In the early hours of the morning he slipped out, not bothering with the usual awkward good-bye that comes in these situations. We knew where we stood.

I showered and went back to bed to sleep off my hangover. Around three in the afternoon, I awoke to the sound of my phone ringing. My mother called to invite me to dinner.

"I have a roast in the oven," she offered. "And those little potatoes you like so much."

"Yeah, okay." The best option I had on my own was a piece of American cheese and a half can of tuna sitting in my fridge. But she didn't need to know my reason for saying yes.

"Are you tired, dear? You sound tired."

"A little."

"I'll put on a pot of coffee for you."

I was about a mile from my parents' house in the left turn lane, waiting for the light to change, when my favorite song came on the radio. "Loser," by Beck. I reached over to turn up the volume and the asshole behind me laid on his horn. Full on blaring, not just a polite beep. The light had turned green and I'd wasted a nanosecond of his life by not pressing the gas pedal immediately. I adjusted my mirror and eased into the turn as if my car wasn't capable of going over ten miles per hour. You should've seen him. Beet red and irate. He even rolled down his window to stick his middle finger out at me. The jackhole burned rubber, fishtailed past me and smashed right into a small dog. The guy didn't even try to swerve. He didn't stop either, just kept on driving as the pup's body flew up and over the car and slammed against the ground, *thunk, thunk.*

I steered over to the side of the road to avoid running over the body. My hands were shaking so hard I could barely get the hazard lights on. I slid out of my car and dashed over to the little guy, my stomach already flip-flopping and I hadn't even seen any blood yet. I held my breath. Surveyed the scene. Not good.

The first thunk was clearly the impact of Mr. Asshole's muscle car bashing into the.. the.. dog? He didn't even look like a dog anymore. His tail was fluffed up to about three times normal, his intestines were seeping half out of his gut, pale and pink with

Animal Husbandry

smears of mottled blood clinging to the exposed parts. His mouth hung open and his purple-black tongue lolled to the side. His left eye was missing, the socket ragged with strands of skin like broken rubber bands.

Without even thinking, I reached for him, pressed his feather light body against mine and choked out the inane things people say in times of duress. "You're going to be okay, buddy. It's going to be fine. You hang on. Stay with me."

I loaded him up in the passenger seat and arranged my jacket around him, trying to keep his insides intact. A strange silence surrounded us, suspending time. In that moment, I realized just how responsible I was for keeping him alive. I'd never felt so important in all my life. Like I had a true purpose for once.

I don't remember the drive to my parents' house or getting out of the car. Just my mother's face when I burst through the door with bits of fur and blood smeared on me. A limp little body in my arms.

My father dropped his newspaper and shot up from his recliner.

"What the hell?" he said.

"Your windbreaker!" my mother shrieked.

I pulled back the sleeve of my jacket covering the carnage. My mother scanned the exposed gut, the dangling tongue, the missing eye. She leaned into my father and started crying, her face splotched red like her blood pressure was up.

"Please, Dale," she whispered, "help him."

"What do you expect me to do here? I can't perform miracles," my father said, rolling up his sleeves.

"You have to save him, Dad!"

"Jesus, Janey. One of these days you're going to have to let me enjoy my retirement." My father went to work pushing intestines back inside Buddy's body and pinching the wound closed. He checked vital signs, examined the empty eye socket, and ordered my mother to fix him a drink.

My mother bee-lined it to the medicine cabinet, gathered needle and suture thread, bandages, and painkillers. She arranged the supplies on the coffee table beside my father, then disappeared into the kitchen to make his drink.

I stood there like a useless limb while my father swabbed and stitched and bandaged Buddy back to life.

"He's lucky. It's not as bad as it looks," my father said.

We were at the dining room table, my mother and I sipping coffee, while my father stirred his cocktail. Buddy, as we had taken to calling him, lay on the couch sedated out of his mind.

"Foxes are actually very resilient," my father said.

"Foxes? He's a fox?" I asked.

My parents exchanged a glance, then turned their patronizing eyes on me.

"You didn't notice?" my father asked, almost laughing.

"He's so dainty," my mother said.

"Strong, though," my father added for my benefit.

Helpless, I thought. I pulled a chair up next to the couch and gazed at Buddy all sewn up and whole again. So helpless. Black sutures curled out of his wounds. Dried blood splattered his face. I traced the outline of his body feeling the way his fur changed texture from coarse to soft. The pads on his feet were well-worn. His face, serene. A fox. How did I miss that?

When Buddy came out of his haze the next morning his face registered confusion. I tried not to crowd him. No doubt he was wondering what the hell had happened for him to wind up on a stranger's couch, feeling beaten and drugged. I couldn't talk over the feelings that welled up inside of me. My father stepped in using his impeccable bedside manner and explained. The more my father talked, the more Buddy squirmed and jerked around. When he started in with a low growl and curled his lips up to bare his teeth, my father reared back and shot him in the arm with a sedative.

"Don't take it personally, Janey. He's disoriented from the pain killers."

On day three of his recovery, Buddy sat up and stretched as if he'd just had a long nap. He surveyed his wounds then hopped down off the couch. He didn't seem to need further explanation. My parents were smiling, my mother leaning into my father again. We had done it, saved him! He was ours to love now without the risk of loss. A total reversal of how love usually works.

A few days later I moved Buddy in with me. My parents didn't say anything about it like they usually would have. My mother gave us some new ace bandages in case we needed them. My father packed up some pain meds and a stack of medical journals.

"Read these. It'll help strengthen that eye," he said, and handed them over to Buddy.

To me, he said, "Watch for infection at the wound sites. Call me if anything changes."

They hugged us both. It was more than they'd ever done for anyone I'd brought home, including that stupid football player I dated in high school just to please them.

Margo came by my apartment. She'd never seen a fox before, except on television. She eyeballed Buddy so intently I felt embarrassed for her. I offered her a margarita and eventually she relaxed enough to move past the novelty of the situation. She sat and visited with us like we were an old married couple. I tried not to feel superior.

Then on our three-month anniversary, Buddy went missing. I was at work with a hell of a respiratory infection, coughing all over my co-workers and wiping my nose raw. I'd used up all my sick days nursing Buddy back to health. My boss finally told me to go home, we'd work something out with the hours. I stopped by Walgreens for Robitussin and a can of chicken noodle soup and when I got home, Buddy wasn't there. I tried not to worry. *Maybe he just needed some fresh air*. I guzzled some Robitussin straight out of the bottle and lay down. I wanted to sit up and wait for him but the elixir took me down against my will.

I woke up to someone ringing my doorbell repeatedly. In a Robitussin-induced haze, I pulled the covers over my head and tried to ignore the sound but whoever it was, wasn't giving up. I got out of bed and stumbled toward the door. A stern-faced cop stood on the other side frowning at me for taking so long to get to him.

"Jane Crowder?"

"Guilty as charged," I said.

The cop didn't appear to appreciate my attempt at humor. His posture softened a little and he took off his hat.

"Ma'am. There's been an incident..." he started.

I knew right off it had to do with Buddy. My first thought was that the asshole who had run over him had come to finish the job, just to piss me off. I'd been on the lookout for that muscle car and that meathead since the day we crossed paths. But what the cop told me was far worse.

He explained that around 3:15 that afternoon a fox had been observed scampering out in traffic at the intersection of Main and

42

Animal Husbandry

7th and was struck by a city bus. The bus driver was unable to make an abrupt stop or swerve to avoid the fox, as it would've put the passengers at risk. Onlookers from both Starbucks and Subway stated they'd seen the fox dart out from a row of nearby hedges, run into the intersection and stop in front of the oncoming bus. According to witnesses, it appeared to be a purposeful act.

I stood there in my robe, my nose dripping, my fists clenched, contemplating what would happen if I grabbed the cop's gun and shot him in the chest for what he said. He launched into the "I'm sorry for your loss" part of his speech. The useless blather that's supposed to make a person feel better after a death. I slammed the door.

I don't recall driving to my parents', but there I was, bursting in on them the same as I had the day I brought Buddy home.

"Janey? What is it?" my father asked. He struggled to get up from his recliner.

The details of the moment held my attention, protecting my mind from the reality of what had happened. My mother's face ashen. The dish of ice cream shaking in her hands. The television blaring an infomercial for a pressure cooker guaranteed to cook an entire meal in ten minutes. My father looking old.

I blurted out what the cop said. Everything. Even though, for a second I considered leaving out the purposeful act part. I didn't want to see my mother cry. Or hear my father harrumph the way he did when it came to illogical things.

"Son of a bitch," he said, "after all we've done for him."

"Such a waste," my mother cried as her shoulders caved in on her. Her ice cream melted into a gooey pool of mush, the nuts succumbing to their weight, drowning.

"I'm sorry," I said. "I thought he was different."

43

My mother stroked my hair and said, "I know, honey. I know. We did, too." But she didn't know how I felt. She had my father. She had my father and always would.

"I'm going to go," I said, suddenly aware I was still in my bathrobe. I squeezed my mother's hand and left.

***

Margo came over a couple of days later. I suspected my parents called her and asked her to stop by to check on me. My place was a disaster; the trash overflowing, balls of Kleenex strewn all over the place, a pile of blankets on the couch where I'd been stationed for the past few days. She offered to clear out anything having to do with Buddy. She'd even brought an empty box.

"How could I have been so stupid?" I asked Margo.

"You are not stupid. How could you know he was suicidal?"

"Well for starters, he jumped out in front of a fast moving car the day I met him."

"But, that was an *accident*."

"No, it wasn't, Margo. I can see that now. You know what really pisses me off about the whole thing? All those times he smiled at me, I thought he was saying thank you and he was really just figuring out how soon he could get rid of me. Everyone I've ever dated has done the exact same thing. Used me, pretended they loved me until they were strong enough to leave. My love is never enough to keep someone around."

Margo placed the long metal pick I'd used on Buddy's hair in the box, on top of my soiled jacket and a roll of unused bandages. I could tell she didn't know what to say. Maybe part of her agreed with me and couldn't come up with a believable rebuttal. I would've argued with her no matter what she said.

For the first time in my life, I preferred to be alone. I started going on long hikes by myself, the more rugged the better. Sometimes I'd get lucky. I'd slip into a meditative state plodding one foot in front of the other and escape from analyzing everything I'd messed up in my life. Other times I'd hear voices, not hallucinations, just voices. My mom saying, "I'm worried about you." Or Margo asking me when I was going to start dating again. Buddy, not saying anything just staring at me as if asking, "Why didn't you just let me die?"

Eight miles, ten miles. No matter how long the hike, it never seemed enough to completely lose myself. Then I found out about this hike, an eighteen-mile loop in the Rocky Mountains that picked up in Estes Park. A week before I planned to go, someone spotted a mountain lion about a half-mile in from the trailhead. The story appeared in the local newspaper. My mother pointed it out to me when I mentioned my hiking plans.

"Sounds dangerous," my mother said, tapping her finger on the article.

"Look, Mom, spotting a mountain lion *in the mountains* is not exactly newsworthy."

"Why don't you postpone a week or two, to be sure?"

She paused, waiting for my father to say something to support her position. She even cleared her throat to make sure he was aware of her waiting.

My father pinched the bridge of his nose and sighed. He cast his eyes down into his coffee cup like it was the damnedest coffee he'd ever seen.

"Leave the girl alone, already. She knows how to handle herself," he said.

"Fine," my mother conceded. "But you better call us the minute you get back."

To be honest, I hoped I didn't run into that mountain lion. I hiked in search of solitude, to reconsider my life's choices without really having to think about them, and to grieve without the hassle of explaining my tears to anyone. In short, I was trying to get my shit together. The last thing I needed was to be distracted by the bad-boy type. I'm sure there are perfectly wonderful mountain lions roaming around, but I have yet to meet one that doesn't at least look like he's ready to devour you.

As it turned out, I didn't see much wildlife on the trail. At least, not initially. A squirrel here and there. Plenty of birds making noise but nothing more. The trail was muddied and slick from the occasional heavy rains that rolled through. I spent the first half of the hike developing a rhythm, steadying my feet and considering my next step.

Look, step, breathe.

Look, step, breathe.

My mind settled in to mull over everything and nothing.

I came out of the thick wooded part of the trail into an open field. Boulders jutted out of the ground, some as big as cars. The sun, which had been trapped behind smeary clouds misting rain on me all morning, burst out and practically blinded me. The change in terrain and weather caused a shift in my mood. I hadn't realized I'd been crying. Hadn't noticed the thin line of blood oozing from my knee where I must've snagged it on a thorny, low-lying vine.

Animal Husbandry

When I reached the first reasonably sized boulder, I plopped down, wiped my eyes and dabbed at the blood that'd almost made it to my sock. I hadn't heard anything for a while, deaf in my own thoughts. Look, step, breathe. Now, I felt the cool of the rock under me, heard the birds screaming out to each other. Cicadas and crickets sawing their legs together. Then, this breathing. A huffing, snorting kind of breathing coming from behind me.

I suppose to some degree I'd been expecting the mountain lion. When I finally worked up the courage to turn, I nearly fell off the rock in surprise. A wooly mammoth. Massive, like a wall of shag carpet tacked up in front of me. His tusks, his trunk, like nothing I'd ever seen. Cracked and smooth, fluid and rough, all at once. The scent of him floated across to me, earthy and musty like sweet patchouli.

His size should've made me feel small and insignificant but instead it empowered me. I felt like I'd been painted right into the landscape alongside him. Like I belonged right there as much a part of the scenery as the giant boulders and the blistering sunlight. He stood rooted to the earth, shifting his head gently in my direction, a small smile of recognition on his face as if we'd known each other for a hundred years and wasn't this something running into each other out here, of all places?

I couldn't bear to say anything, afraid my words would ruin the tenderness of the moment. Instead I listened to the hum of the wind through the open field, the birds whistling into the concrete sky, my heart slowing in my chest.

He loped in closer, turning his head so that one perfectly round eye the size of my fist studied me with interest. The silence between us felt natural. Beautiful, even. He shifted his weight and lurched forward a couple of steps. I sat still on the rock, hoping

47

that if he lumbered away into the horizon I could burn his image in my memory to touch on later as a reminder that certain things do exist. I would've been content in the memory of him, but he stopped in his tracks and lifted his face skyward, waiting. I recognized it as a question. *Are you coming?*

I slid off the rock as if I had no choice in the matter. The universe was summoning me, showing me how all the places I'd been, all the lovers I'd had prior to this moment were necessary in order for me to appreciate this exact moment for what it was. I saw how I'd been avoiding real love to nurse the damaged and sick in exchange for feeling needed. I sidled up beside him, breathed in the scent of oil on his body, the dead grass and cattails and burs adorning him. Together, we climbed until the path got too narrow for him and too steep for me. I held onto his fur for support as we descended the mountains. He stopped a few times when he could sense I needed a rest, and draped his trunk around my shoulders when the sun went down.

"I've met someone," I told my father when he answered the phone.

"Hang on a minute," he said. He jostled the phone and I could hear my mother in the distance instructing him on how to use the speaker feature on his cell phone. More jostling, a few numbers being pressed, then both of their voices sounding like they were talking into a tin can.

"Oh, Janey, not the mountain lion!" My mother said.

"What? No," I started with the usual defensiveness but toned it down when I thought about the way my day had unfolded.

"Who, then?" My father asked.

"You're not going to believe me," I said.

Animal Husbandry

"Janey…" My father's voice rang loud through the line. No doubt he'd gotten his face too close to the phone in an effort to be heard. "Listen, your mother and I are still a little concerned about you after the… the thing with Buddy…and…"

"A wooly mammoth," I interrupted. "I met a wooly mammoth." The truth seemed like the best way to keep from hurting them anymore than I already had.

"But, they're extinct," my father said barely above a whisper.

"That's what I thought, too. But they're not. They're just very private. Reclusive, even."

"Well, I'll be damned," my father said, back in the bottom of the tin can.

"Are you sure you're ready, Janey?" My mother had recovered slightly from her initial alarm but her voice still quivered with uncertainty.

"Yes, Mom."

"Janey," my father said.

"He's a good guy, Dad."

"You're sure?" They said in unison.

"Yeah, I'm sure. This time I'm really sure."

Who We Belong To

I spent the better part of last week deciding whether to kill myself or ride up to the new Dollar General. I sat on the fence about it for a few days, mulled over those coupons they mailed out. *Grand Opening! $5 off every $25 spent!* I didn't have twenty-five dollars to spend but I went anyway. Thought, what the hell. Maybe I'd run into Auby or Hickey. It didn't much matter to me, just as long as I ran into somebody instead of sitting around the trailer scratching my balls in the heat waiting for the fan to oscillate back in my direction. I couldn't take much more of Daisydog either, flopped on the linoleum staring up at me with her hungry pitiful eyes. I figured maybe with it being the grand opening and all, I could pick up some kibble cheap. But I wasn't holding my breath about that.

You ask me, the Dollar General's prices aren't good at all. Not like the Buck Hut where everything is just one dollar, believe it or not. Take the toy section. I could go in there, buy Jordie a few things to play with in the bathtub, a couple picture books about animals, a balloon, a pair of socks, a snickers bar, and never spend more than ten bucks. You'd have thought I'd spent a hundred the way Jordie hugged on me whenever I came home from the Buck Hut. I'd been meaning to take him up there to pick something out himself, just never got around to it.

Anyway, I knew if I ran into Hickey I'd have to listen to him jaw on about this or that like he always did. Mainly he'd complain about being in hot water with the Judge for not paying his child support again. Sometimes all his yammering-on aggravated me. Other times it made me feel better about my own life situation. After listening to Hickey I'd think, at least I don't have all that to worry over. If I was having to find a ride to town every other month to face ol' Judge Haywood and explain why I hadn't paid my child support – I believe I would go on and kill myself. No question there.

As it was, me and Mandy weren't even together anymore so kids weren't an option. At least not between me and her. She's got Jordie but he isn't mine. Tell you the truth, I'm not sure Mandy knows who he belongs to. She doesn't let on like she knows, just says she doesn't want to talk about all that. Jordie's five. Since no guy ever came sniffing around looking for him the whole time Mandy and me were together, I figure it's nothing to lose sleep about. Whoever he is, he doesn't care much about Jordie.

When Mandy broke it off with me, I didn't see it coming. Jordie was sitting there rolling his matchbox truck back and forth on this piece of curled up linoleum in the kitchen, making car noises like usual. I poured Mandy a sweet tea and squeezed some lemon in it like she likes, then I started in on my six-pack. I should've known something was up when she didn't touch her drink. I can be slow to catch on that way.

Looking back on it, she was real quiet that day. She's always quiet but that day she hardly said a word. She said something like, "I can't go on like this, Tripp. I have Jordie to think about." Up to about a month before Mandy said this, I had been finding work every time I turned around. Landing jobs here and there, getting paid decent under the table. So at first when Mandy said she was pulling up stakes, I didn't get her reasoning. But, when I took a step back, saw Jordie pushing that little truck around and seen

Who We Belong To

how Mandy was staring at him like he hung the moon, I could see her point.

With Mandy gone, I didn't have much reason to bust my ass looking for work. Daisydog could scare up something to eat if she had to, and I didn't have much of an appetite. Especially when I thought about the trailer being empty of the little noises Jordie made, or my bed being empty of Mandy.

The first night after Mandy left I woke up to Jordie crying, calling out, Tripp! Tripp! I ran out to the couch expecting to find him sitting up rubbing tears out of his eyes. My heart was pumping in my throat but my damn legs were still asleep. I about kicked over the coffee table trying to get to him. Empty beer bottles went clanking up against one another. They ended up all over the place, spilling the last bit that never wants to come out. I pawed at the couch trying to grab Jordie up in my arms and came up with nothing but his little blanket. Just some old tattered throw I'd had around that Jordie had claimed as his. It still smelled like him, sweet and sour with little kid sweat.

I stayed there a long while thinking up ways to win Mandy back. Hell I even came up with a plan solid enough that I was able to fall back to sleep. When I woke up a few hours later with a goddamn couch spring pressing into my ribcage, I realized then my grand plan was nothing more than loneliness conspiring with the blackest part of the night. I couldn't help it, I started crying thinking about how Mandy wouldn't be sitting on the rocking chair on the porch, sipping on her sweet tea, her hair a mess from tossing around in the bed with me. I hadn't cried like that in fifteen almost sixteen years.

I drove up to the Dollar General. I *did* run into Hickey. He was haggling with the cashier over how she'd rung his order up wrong. Poor girl. Here it was her first day on the register with live customers and ol' Hickey's rattling her chains.

"Jesus, Hickey, give the girl a break already."

I clapped him on the shoulder to say hello and to snap him out of it. I about broke his scrawny body in half hitting him as hard as I did, but it worked. He jerked around in my direction, stopped staring a hole in that girl as if every problem in the world was her doing. She probably thought he was rabid the way spit was gathering at the corner of his mouth. She couldn't know that was his usual.

"It's highway fucking robbery," Hickey said.

"Well, next time don't buy anything," I said. "Ain't no law that says you've got to shop here."

Hickey fixed his eyes back on that girl, but I know he heard me because he snatched his receipt out of her hand and stuffed it down his pants pocket. Then he clawed his bag off the counter and made for the exit. I went behind him, shaking my head so the girl would see I didn't agree with the way he was handling the situation. Once we were outside, Hickey let loose about what really had him so tore up.

"I'm fixin' to go to jail tomorrow because of them people," he said.

He was chawing on a Milky Way bar like he hadn't eaten a day in his life, half of it spilling out of his mouth when he talked.

"Them people? You mean your kids?"

"The way Rhonda Sue carries on, I ain't even sure they *are* my kids. She acts like she hates my goddamn guts."

I could tell he'd been thinking about his situation for several hours by the time I ran into him. Once he got on the subject of Rhonda Sue, there was no stopping him. I'd been told she spent a good amount of her time bitching about Hickey. A match made in Heaven.

"Me dropping off Huggies don't mean a damn thing to the Judge. He wouldn't care if I nursed 'em at my own tit." Hickey puffed out his chest and dropped his voice low to do his best impression of the Judge. "Just pay your support in full, Mr. Hickey and we won't have to meet down here at the court house like we have been."

Hickey went back to slouching, like a kid that's been hollered at. "He don't care that Rhonda Sue won't use that money on the kids, she'll spend it on herself and laugh all the way to the bank when the next check comes."

I let Hickey prattle on, knowing he was just blowing off steam. He needed to get all that off his chest before he headed to court, especially if Rhonda Sue brought Ray-Ray Jr. and Brittany to court with her. Everybody knew it was for effect. Cute little buggers. Blue-eyed and red-headed. No mistaking who they belonged to.

For all the spouting off Hickey was doing outside the Dollar General, I knew he'd play it quiet at the courthouse. He was afraid of the Judge just like the rest of us. Hell, Judge knew what trouble you'd wind up in before that trouble even found you. If you didn't take advantage of "the opportunities available to you," as he called them, he would throw your ass in jail for a few days to let you marinate on the error of your ways.

"That old son of a bitch thinks he can just tell everybody settin' up in that courthouse to get a job," Hickey said. "Like it's some easy thing to do in this piss-ant town. I'd like to see him get a job that easy."

"He's got a job, Hick. A pretty decent one at that."

"He acts like I'm settin' up here enjoying being broke all the goddamn time. Like I don't *want* to work. How's he know I'm not trying, Tripp? Huh?"

"He knows. Everybody knows. Word gets around."

The door to the Dollar General opened and closed. Hickey jerked his head to the side and got a dirty look in on the cashier.

"Hey," I said, "you seen Auby lately?"

"Not if I can help it." Hickey laughed like it was the first time he'd said this.

Auby is Hickey's half-stupid cousin. I don't say it to be mean. He fell out of a tree some years back and landed on his head. He'd scaled up a tulip tree chasing after a cat who didn't care to be caught. Hickey told me Auby kept on climbing well past the point he ought to, then shimmied out onto a branch where that cat sat swishing her tail at him. The branch broke and Auby fell, the arms on that old tulip tree tried to catch his fat little body but missed. Hickey said he never saw so much blood come out of a person's head before or since. Auby went stupid after that. Hickey and I have spent more than a few afternoons considering whether that boy wasn't a bit slow to begin with.

Tell you the truth, I was glad I hadn't been around to see that mess. A sight like that sticks with me more than it ought to. I got about three things stuck in my mind at all times, depending on what's going on in my life. Some of them strong enough to make me contemplate not sticking around. The day I went to the Dollar General, I carried with me the repeating image of Mandy asleep next to me in nothing but her panties and a t-shirt, her face mushed up in the pillow. A peaceful sight as far as that goes, until I factored in she'd left me.

Second, and I'm not sure this doesn't qualify as a bigger deal, was this image of Jordie. His face glowing with a smile so big his eyes disappeared, his little hands holding onto his latest matchbox car. Several times a day since Mandy left I'd hear him call for me to come play with him. And the thing of it was I'd get up from whatever I was doing and look for him until I realized he was gone.

In between Mandy and Jordie popping into my mind were these snippets of my little brother Birdy and me playing catch the day he died. This has been stuck in my mind for going on sixteen years, playing like a picture reel, running all the damn time in the background of my life.

Somewhere in the middle of Hickey complaining about having two kids to take care of, I caught the memory of Birdy—that same damn memory, the day he died.

It always starts the same. First the scent of leather oil floats on the air and I can hear Birdy plunking a baseball into his new glove. Then, I see myself throwing that final pop fly. The ball goes in the air so high that the sun swallows it up and makes it invisible. I call out, "Go long," even though it's baseball we're playing and not football. Birdy yells, "I got it! I got it!" He ambles backward, squints his freckled face up at the sky. I see every inch of his six-year-old face, his long eyelashes catching the sunlight, his little bitty nose flaring with the excitement of doing the thing he loves best. The ball falls from the sky looking like it's coming straight at me and steals my attention away from Birdy. At first I don't notice him inching backward toward the kettle of boiling oil on the fire pit behind him.

The ball lands. Birdy's heels catch on the stones around the fire pit. His face changes from grinning and squinting to wide-eyed surprise. He jerks his arms back to break his fall and lands hard against the pot. The cast iron handle clangs against its potbelly as the whole thing tilts. Oil sizzles against the hot rocks. Then flames whoosh, leaping and engulfing Birdy. The heat from the flames slaps my face. Someone's screaming, a deafening noise, then silence. My body is numb, immovable. I'm frozen in the sound of my brother being burned alive.

Ma comes tearing across the lawn with the hose in her hand and starts spraying before she even gets to the fire. She's yelling at me but I can't hear her, can only see her mouth moving. The veins in her neck bulging. Her slipper in the grass behind her.

Orange and red shapes dance higher and higher into the air. My hands are on Birdy. I pull at him. I lose my grip against his skin, melted into his clothes, crusted and curled, hanging and dripping off the bone. Still bubbling. I squeeze harder as the flames lick my arms and shoot up toward my chest. I hold on until Birdy is out of the fire and in the grass. Ma's beside me grunting, slapping at the flames with her apron. Birdy's skin latches onto the apron and stretches in long threads. Then everything around me goes gray. The colors of the flames disappear. The blue of my mother's eyes are drained and turn ashen. Forever.

I know that this memory is mine to carry. The events of that day belong to me as much as Hickey's kids belong to him. I've got to answer for that day. The difference is I've got to face myself, not the Judge. I can't say who is harder, but I can guess.

Hickey'd been squeezing that Milky Way wrapper in his fist the whole time he was talking, flattening it down to near nothing with his frustration. He looked down at it in his hand, sort of surprised that it was there, and chucked it into the parking lot. The wrapper skittered across the blacktop, catching on a breeze, twisting this way and that way. Made me think; ain't that life for you? Getting squeezed, thrown and caught on a breeze, never quite sure where you'll end up. Could be outside the Dollar General, could be worse.

"I best get moving," I said. I could hardly get the words out. I no more than got my key in the car door when Hickey called out, "Hey, where's Mandy?"

I eased into my seat, hoping to God he wouldn't come stand by my window and carry on about Mandy not being with me. He might've said something more but I couldn't hear him over the rub of metal on metal as I yanked the door closed. That old Dodge was about sound proof once the doors were closed and the windows were up. The silence made me deaf for a second, then came Birdy clamping his glove open and shut like he did a thousand times to break it in. I clunked the car into gear and rolled on out of the parking lot. As soon as I hit Highway 50 and got my windows rolled down, I started to feel a little better.

I'd been up and down that stretch of 50 so many times, the car about drove itself. I pulled against the steering wheel when my turn came up just to keep it from driving straight to the trailer. I cruised out along the two-lane highway, just under the speed limit, focusing on little things; the road cut between rocky shale walls. The tiny waterfalls spilling out here and there. The trees gathered up like bunches of broccoli. The clouds thick with the threat of rain.

I was on autopilot, my brain telling my body what to do without me even having to think. I got to wishing it could stay that way, me not having to decide anything, just sit there at the wheel and watch the world go by. But sometimes I didn't much like what the world slung at me.

Before I knew it, the car took me by Mandy's Meemaw's house, where Mandy was staying. I drove by, released the gas so as to roll past without being noticed. Jordie was out in the yard, whacking at the grass with a stick, his little ball cap on backwards. Mandy was watching him from the porch. She had on jean shorts with the front cuffed up. They showed off her tanned legs.

At the sight of the two of them my mind stopped working. I stepped on the brakes, then gunned it, then went back to the brakes hard. All that indecision made it look like the old Dodge couldn't make up its damn mind what to do. Mandy quick turned her head toward the road and Jordie followed suit. When he realized it was me he waved with all his might. Hell I had no choice but to turn around and pull into Meemaw's driveway.

Mandy smiled polite at me as I cut the engine off. She raised her eyebrows a little like maybe she was glad to see me. I could hardly get out the door before Jordie ran up to the car, squinting his eyes up at me against the sun coming out. He called my name about a dozen times, Tripp! Tripp! Tripp!

I came out careful not to knock the little fella over with the car door. He latched onto my thigh like he'd always done. Mandy hugged me around the neck quick and stood there as pretty as ever. It about took my legs out from under me when I remembered we weren't together anymore. I steadied myself against the Dodge and tried to look casual.

"I hope you don't mind I stopped by," I said.

"No, it's fine," Mandy said. She stared down at Jordie still clinging to my leg. "He's been missing you."

The sun dipped behind a stack of white clouds and the air went cool. Before long Mandy said, "Jordie, run on inside and get Tripp a coke. Get yourself one, too." Jordie didn't need to be told twice when it came to having a Coca-Cola.

Mandy and me leant against the car, her real close next to me on her own doing. I got the feeling she was waiting for me to say something. But I'm no good in that department so I said nothing.

Who We Belong To

I didn't have a real plan and anything I'd entertained up to that point didn't seem to fit the situation. Finally, I decided to reach over and take her hand. When I did, she didn't pull away.

"Well," I said. Then I just stood there trying to figure out what to do next.

"If you and Jordie want, I thought we could take a ride up to the Buck Hut."

Just then Jordie came running out the front door with a Coke in each hand. He had them all shook up by the time he got to me.

"Thank you sir," I said.

The formality of it must've tickled him some because he laughed. He held up both his coke and mine and waited on me to open them. I handed him my keychain with the bottle opener on it and said, "You try." The way he went jumping around in excitement you'd a thought I'd given him the keys to my car and asked him to drive. He tried but he couldn't get the bottles open so I went on and popped the tops off. He drunk about half his in three swallows.

"Get your shoes on, Jordie," Mandy said. "Tripp's taking us up to the store."

Next thing I know, we're piled up in the car and I'm steering that old Dodge toward the Buck Hut.

Teddy's Dead

My father lay on the ground of what used to be Foy's Junkyard. Dead. Nude. The holes in his body leaking fluid. I don't want to know how they got him here from the hospital, where I saw him last. We aren't allowed to know. We're only told when he dies, when to be at the gate, and how long we can stay. Others who've been through this tell us to bring masks. Burn incense. Use Castille Soap. I gather all of these things for Mom and me before Dad dies. I feel prepared, ready for my impending role as man of the house. The Advisor calls and announces, "Time of death: 8:17am. Burial: 12:30pm. Allotted time: fifteen minutes." I hang up. Tell Mom. I am no longer prepared.

The call means Dad didn't succumb to a bedside conversion, though I know the offer is extended in unimaginable ways. He could do it, declare himself a Believer seconds before he dies. He could be dressed in his pinstriped suit, wearing his only tie. He could be laid in a casket with a silk pillow under his head, friends and family hunched over him weeping. Mom and I could be sitting among arranged flowers, holding hands, listening to whispered remembrances of my father. These comforts carry a high price tag.

If Dad converts, Mom and me would be shuttled to separate interview rooms and invited to confess the error of our ways. We'd be offered Salvation, a chance to avow belief. In exchange for our conversion, the Administrators would burn our belongings and move us to the other end of town, where the Believers live. Not the quiet Believers who nod in your direction and say, "Have a blessed day," but the loud preachy talkers who have been instructed to watch you closely for signs of reversion or relapse. We'd be provided with one-size fits all clothing and the gray vest with an embroidered "C" on the back. The C stands for Crossover and signifies to everyone that we made a last minute conversion. We will need to be watched until we earn our "B" for Believer. We'd be assigned to our first new job. *IF THE DEATH OF A LOVED ONE PROMPTS A CONVERSION, THE NEWLY CONVERTED WILL BE ASSIGNED TO THE MAINTENANCE OF THE BURIAL MOUND FOR NO LESS THAN ONE YEAR.* I already know the school district will not hold my position for a year. Art teachers aren't exactly hard to do without.

The Friday before Dad dies he's having a good day, able to sit up and sip a little bone broth the nurse brings him. He smiles at her, absently reaches into his robe pocket for cigarettes that haven't been there for years. "Eat," she tells Dad. To me, she says, "Five more minutes," then steps out into the hallway. The door closes behind her. *NON-BELIEVERS ARE TO BE ASSIGNED THEIR OWN DUTY NURSE WHO SHALL REMAIN BEDSIDE AT ALL TIMES TO BEAR WITNESS SHOULD A CONVERSION OCCUR.* The broken rule makes me nervous, giddy.

"You'll be tempted," Dad says. He's wearing his stern teacher face. "Don't do it for me. Give it a couple of weeks. See how you feel then. But, don't do it for me. Stay strong. For your mother." His face melts into memories that have little to do with me.

I nod, stifle tears with a cough.

"Don't pay attention to their rhetoric. Subscribing to reincarnation is just asking to die over and over again. Why

Teddy's Dead

would anyone want to do that? Once is enough for me." Dad fiddles with the IV port, scratches under a corner of the tape pressed over the needle. "Now, if I got a say in it, maybe then I'd sign up for the afterlife." He peels back the tape further, scratches the skin closer to the needle. "I'd be Teddy Roosevelt."

Hardly a surprising choice from a man who taught American history for twenty-two years.

"Or Abe Lincoln. Good ol' honest Abe."

"Get shot in the back of the head? Really, Dad?"

"Sure. Why not?"

"Well, for one, it might be painful."

"Like this isn't?" he says. He pushes the tape back down, smoothes it over the needle with his thumb and forefinger. It curls back up.

I look at the door, make sure it's still closed.

"You know who I'd choose? Not the first go around, maybe the third or fourth time around? Hitler. Definitely Hitler."

"Hitler? Jesus, Dad. Hitler?"

"Come on, Brian. Don't you ever wonder what ran through Hitler's mind?" Dad says and reaches into his pocket for the cigarettes again.

"Sure, but I think I'd rather just be his friend. Let him tell me over a cup of coffee."

"No, no, no, Brian. You've got to be inside his head, not next to it. Otherwise you're just witnessing history, not *being* history."

The nurse pushes through the door, jangling a few pills against a paper cup in her hand.

My father drops to a whisper, "You can't expect to always be the good guy, Brian. That's the problem. If there is an afterlife, you're going to have to be the asshole sometimes. It's a roll of the dice, the chance you've got to take."

65

"Time's up," the nurse says.

I get up, stand beside Dad. "See you on the other side," I whisper and manage a smile.

"Over my dead body," he says. Chokes out a raspy laugh.

The nurse shushes him.

Mom and I are in place behind the taped line. The front loader clunks into gear and lurches forward. The squeal of the brakes does little to cover up the sound of my mother sobbing. She hands me the rose, "You do it," she says. *NON-BELIEVERS ARE ALLOTED ONE ROSE PER DESCENDENT.* I throw our single rose. It lands hard and skitters up next to Dad's arm; blood red against his flesh.

The bucket of the front loader comes alive. Swinging at its hinges, the claws of the bucket stab into the ground beside Dad. The packed earth crumbles against the persistence of the machine. My father is swallowed up inside the dirt filled bucket and I lose sight of him for a second, lose my ability to breathe.

The machine jerks to a stop and rocks the bucket. The force of the motion rolls Dad on his side. His reappearance brings mom to tears. She swallows a sob and turns her head back toward the gate. No one else is here. It's the rule. Only immediate family are allowed at burials. We are told this is for safety reasons. But I know it's a tactic used to create a façade of loneliness, to make us think we are the only non-Believers left. I have to hand it to the Administrators. Watching your dead loved one get scooped up by a contraption and dropped onto a pile of decaying bodies is an effective method for invoking change.

It does a number on Mom. The smell alone could cause a conversion. The masks aren't helping. Rotting flesh permeates. The Castile soap is at home waiting as is the patchouli incense.

Teddy's Dead

Patchouli is the only incense rumored to eradicate the smell. When Dad had gotten worse, I went to a friend of mine who had connections to the black market. Matt got me ten sticks, no charge. "I liked your old man. Even though he failed me in American History."

I remember that time like it's last week instead of ten years ago. This is before the Administrators take over. Before they enact curfews and ban home visits. Back then, you could socialize at will. Had I known the changes to come, I would've taken advantage of that, despite my introverted tendencies.

Matt comes by and stays for dinner, as usual. During dinner, my father glares at Matt, steers the topic toward history any chance he gets. As he passes a mountain of whipped white potatoes with butter, he can't resist. "Do you know about the potato famine the Irish suffered through?" Matt shakes his head, stares at my father unaware he's about to be hit with hard facts.

After Matt leaves, and I swallow down my embarrassment, I say, "Not everybody cares about history as much as you, Dad."

"Well, they ought to care. If they want to understand just how much history repeats itself," Dad says. "You want to know how to avoid making the same mistakes over and over again? First you have to be informed. Get the facts. Then and only then can you form an opinion. A solid opinion, Brian, not the trend of the day. You never blindly follow any institution, be it education, government, or religion." A by-product of the sixties, Dad has a 'question everything' attitude at his core. And he beats the drum loudly, only it's to the wrong crowd. High school kids just don't care. Back when I was sixteen, all I cared about was where to score a joint and how to make history with Maryanne Walker.

The front loader pops into gear and rolls toward the dead. I avoid focusing on the mass, avoid breathing deeply. But now with my father poised above it, I take it in. Flies gather at the top of the heap, land on discernable bodies with recognizable faces. Further down the pile, flesh melts into ribbons of color, creams and peaches, browns and greys. Liquids, ooze and drip, slide like miniature waterfalls from a rock wall. Birds caw overhead in irregular rhythms. Fingers curl gently in half-closed fists. Arms and legs bend and flop in awkward poses. Faces sag and droop. Eyes leak out of their sockets and puddle at the bottom of the heap. Ass cheeks deflate and belly buttons protrude. Aunt Alice is in there somewhere, closer to the bottom. I search for her lily-white skin and silver-black hair. Hair has turned into tumbleweed caught up in rocks. All a delightful ploy to get me to believe.

The bucket bends and expels Dad. He falls head first, top heavy from the gas and fluids filling his torso. Mom squeezes my arm. She's trembling. I turn my face up toward the camera mounted on the gate and grind my jaw against the words inside my mouth. I rip my mask off, wad it up in my fist and chuck it on the ground in front of me.

"Brian," Mom sobs. "Don't!"

This sort of outrage is not tolerated, even at funerals. *ANY DIRECT OR INDIRECT THREAT OF REVOLT WILL RESULT IN IMMEDIATE DEATH.* Though it's not stated, the preferred method is decapitation. I've seen it happen for less than what I've just done. I bend over and scoop it up in my hand, shove it down in my pocket, like it was an accident.

The machine clunks into reverse and rolls away from the scene. A slight man steps out from the cab and lopes over to the gate, avoiding contact. He hangs his head, clears his throat. The timer shows three minutes remaining.

Teddy's Dead

"Let's go," I say through gritted teeth. I steer Mom toward the exit, hold her by the elbow as she leans into me. As we near the camera I straighten up tall and trod toward the gate. Mom lets go of my arm, squares up her shoulders and we strut out of there with as much conviction as we can muster in our weakened knees.

At home someone has spray painted the front door in large bubble letters, *NONBELIEVER*. I've seen worse than the truth painted on a door. An involuntary snorting laugh escapes me. This is the work of the radicals. The same assholes that have made it necessary to keep the gate locked. The morons who think it's a good idea to light the pile on fire every few months, as if they can make the dead deader. Not a very clever bunch.

Mom and I take turns showering and lighting incense. She takes two Valium and goes to her bedroom. When I'm sure she's asleep, I paint over the *NONBELIEVERS* with a half-gallon of primer I find in the garage. I scout around the perimeter of the house. Next to the back door is a small *BE SAVED*. I paint over that too. I take a couple of Mom's Valium and lay on the couch.

In the space between rest and sleep, my mind takes me back to my father. In his final 'screw you' to the establishment, he nose-dives into the bodies of his fellow kind, disappears into the colors and textures, the bones and the skin of a hundred others before him. He swims to the bottom, pushes off and breaks through the surface. He climbs to the top, and balances on the torsos underfoot. He clasps his hands over his head, straightens his arms and legs, points his toes and slices back into the pool beneath him. Down and back, down and back, the bodies rippling against his movement. The last time he comes up for air he shakes his straggling hair to the side and leans back into a float. His face is serene as the sun kisses his cheeks. He gives a small ankle kick to keep from slipping under. He waves, rests his arms behind his head. Why won't he close his eyes? I want him to close his eyes.

I wake up, sweaty and groggy, breathing heavy. Mom is still asleep in the same position I left her. Her chest rises and falls in the evenness of drugged slumber. In a flash, I see her inside the bucket of the front loader, with her eyes closed and her pale body being cast about. Her eyelids flutter and bring me back to the unreality of the day's events. She's less worn in her sleep. Her beauty is restored and she is once again my father's love.

I step outside, consider lighting a cigarette. Some of the letters of NONBELIEVERS have bled through the primer, leaving a random display of bent black curves disappearing into white space. It reminds me of the artwork of one of my students. He paints in black, mixes in white to create various shades of gray. His paintings are a testimony to endless shadow and depth. The kind of thing I'd studied in college but never quite accomplished.

I light the cigarette and start the two-mile trek to the dead pile, figuring I have plenty of time to talk myself out of going. But I lose track of time inside the trepidation. I'm outside the gate, searching for my father, his sparse gray hair and bloated body. He's on his side, one arm resting beneath his head, just as we'd left him. He stares out at me as if he's been expecting my visit.

"What else have I got to do?" his facial expression seems to say.

I grab at the fencing, poke my fingers through the openings to have something to hang on to. I clear my throat.

"Are you sure about this, Dad?"

He doesn't say anything. Doesn't move a muscle.

"You could be Teddy Roosevelt right now. Or…"

The wind carries a few strands of his hair back and forth across his face. He doesn't blink.

Teddy's Dead

"…Lincoln."

The crows start up like sirens, yelling at me, yelling at each other.

"Hitler?" I start crying then. My eyes burn from the stench.

"Impossible. Trust me on this," he says with his eyes turned toward the camera. A fly crawls out of his mouth. "Go sit with your mother. Now." I let go of the fence, wipe my face, and glare into the camera. Is it even on? Of course it is, it's always on.

When I get back to the house I walk around to the back door. *BE SAVED* is completely covered. The sun has baked the primer on.

Thirteen Years

On the other side of my cubicle Barb was telling José her latest conspiracy theory.

"The government, the CDC, the World Health Organization, they're all lying to us," Barb said in her crackled, mannish voice. She's a smoker. The kind of smoker who only gets out of bed every morning because her nicotine-laden body demands more. Then she caffeinates herself to the point of intoxication and mistakes that for being awake. About a hundred cigarettes later she's outside my cube telling José the real reason the flu virus is so rampant this year.

It's a welcome change, the new theory. It means we're finally freed from hearing about the last one; the real reason the levees broke in Louisiana. Thanks to the media, Barb held on to that theory for weeks after Hurricane Katrina hit. The day she broke the news of that theory I almost lost it.

"The Feds knew those levees wouldn't hold and they decided to do nothing," Barb said. "Why?" she asked this rhetorical question during the introduction of each new theory. "Because the Feds knew the only people that wouldn't survive would be poor Blacks."

"*What?*" I asked and then cursed myself for showing interest. How many weeks will that set her back, I wondered. Worse yet, my question invited her to pop her head over my cube wall and drive her research home.

"Think about it, Scott. None of the poorest, blackest, residents were evacuated. Not even the invalids" – which she pronounced as "in-vlids – "who were on their death beds in nursing homes. Those people died, drowned, because their White nurses and White doctors were flown out or bussed out way before the storm hit." She raised her over-arched eyebrows in my direction, latched her bony fingers over the cube, and waited for my reaction.

Barb watched the news every night and reported back in the morning about what she saw. Images of people on rooftops spelling out HELP, wading through debris waist high, being pulled into canoes, and dead bodies bloated and floating in the streets. All of them Black, she pointed out with her words and her finger. Always that finger was pointing.

As usual, whenever Barb faced me, José rolled his eyes behind her back. When she turned to José, I would look away, hopeful that when she turned back around she'd see that I was busy sifting through my warrants. In Barb's seventeen-year history with the county, the warrant pile had never gone away, so she didn't take notice like I hoped. José agreed to whatever Barb said but only to spur her on. Getting Barb riled up fit in nicely with José's philosophy about not working too hard.

On day fifteen of the Real Reason the Levees Broke Conspiracy, I miscalculated Barb's ability to succumb to logic. I said, "I'm sure plenty of White people died too, Barb."

"The hell they did!" Barb yelled. "Show me the numbers, Scott. Show me."

José laughed and pointed at me while Barb shot daggers out from under her sagging eyelids.

Since the floodgates were already opened, so to speak, I said, "Do you think the Feds engineered the hurricane, too? Deployed it like a missile straight at New Orleans?"

Thirteen Years

My wife, Marnie, and I had had a blowout one morning about my ever-increasing tendency to bitch about work. She yipped at me and said that thirteen more years until retirement was practically nothing and I should be thankful for a paying job, with good benefits and retirement *especially in this economy.* I barked back at her and said thirteen more years chained to a desk in an office full of lunatics was about the worst torture I could imagine. By the time I got into the office I was ready to call Marnie and tell her all the things I was sick of hearing *her* bitch about. But instead I started in on Barb, forgetting that you can't argue with crazy.

Barb was less than amused by my questions. Her face turned a blotchy red-white like she wasn't breathing. Her eyes turned into an opaque jade color with nothing inside. The way she clutched the top of my cube, I thought she might be having a heart attack. I'd seen the look plenty of times but not in relation to me.

"Shart," she bellowed, "you're lucky I like you."

She called me Shart because that's what was printed on my badge. It's a combination of my first and last name, Scott Hart. About a week after I started working with her she told me that a shart is a cross between a shit and a fart. I tolerated it from her because it was better than being on her bad side. It didn't take me long to see what kind of special hell Barb unleashed on those who upset her.

As the news of the Katrina disaster wound down I thought we might have a chance of getting past it. But then on day twenty, Barb came in heavy with how the government had put all the remaining, surviving Blacks into a sports arena with no provisions and no hope of rescue.

"No food. No water. It might as well be the Jews in the holocaust," she announced. "It's like an experiment, a psychological experiment. Like the Tuskegee experiment. Fucking Feds."

What did the Jews have to do with Hurricane Katrina, I thought. Marnie and I had gotten past our fight by then so I was able to keep my thoughts to myself that time.

"What is the Tuskegee experiment?" José asked.

While Barb started at the top of that topic, I reached for the ear buds that Marnie had given me for my birthday. The Pixies were singing in my ears while I thumbed through my warrant list. Martin Welsh was on there again for six parole violations. I liked Martin, the dumbass.

Barb loomed over my cube wall and said something in between songs.

"What?" I asked, pulling one ear bud out.

"Don't let Ronnie catch you with those headphones or we'll all be getting another memo about company policy."

"Fuck Ronnie and his memos," José shot across the wall.

That always got Barb going on her absolute favorite topic; how much she hated Ronnie and how he was out to get her. It was a typical work issue about how the boss is a dick. But as usual with Barb, she put her own spin on it.

"I hate that fucking asshole and it's not because he's Black. He'll tell you that's why I hate him but it has nothing to do with it." Barb followed that up with a chronicle of each and every one of the Black men she screwed, up to and including Jerome. Jerome claimed he was the ex-body guard of Jean-Claude Van Damme. What he was doing as a bouncer at the Tin Roof in Detroit never seemed to cross Barb's mind.

"…and Jerome," she laughed up some gravel. "He's not the only guy I had sex with in a bar, but that's not the point of the

76

story." She had her unlit cigarette between her fingers like a pacifier dangling from a baby's bib.

I hated the Jerome Story because in it she was falling down drunk, not wanting to leave the bar at closing time, and Jerome offered to drive her home. He ended up bending her over the bar and the rest was the history that she would repeat proudly a hundred thousand times before she died. Oh, the romance of it all. It was sad, really, but Barb didn't see it. She was such a scrambled mess of mismatched Goodwill clothing and thinning hair and wanna-be biker chick. I couldn't stand to think of her getting plugged at the bar by some bouncer claiming to have ties to Jean-Claude Van Damme, of all people. But, that was not the point of the story.

She capped off at Jerome, though. As if she either stopped having sex after that or switched to another race. I'm not sure which it was, and I never asked. I refused to ask Barb anything about her sex life. Ever. It was one of the few rules I had at work.

Barb circled back around to her hatred for Ronnie and her personal conspiracy theory of why he was out to get her. Secretly, the way she made a case against him made me think she had a thing for Ronnie. They could've been screwing for all I knew or cared. I wouldn't have put it past Ronnie. He used to be the warden at the jail. Plenty of guys I picked up on warrants told me what a low-life Ronnie was. Even the criminals were disgusted by him. And here Ronnie was my boss. Would be for the next thirteen years.

When Barb started in about the H1N1 Conspiracy – I couldn't find my ear buds. I was stuck listening to her and feeling slightly intrigued. The beginning of a theory was always the most entertaining. It went downhill steeply from there.

"The H1N1 is nothing more than the government's botched attempt at targeted germ warfare," she said, rehearsed. She was in a walking cast from the knee down from a nasty fall she took during the last ice storm that hit. She hadn't showered since she fell and could only wear the one pair of pants that fit over the cast. I turned my mind away from the places her body odor was coming from. An image of her and Jerome jogged into my brain. The search for my ear buds turned frantic.

"Who was the germ warfare aimed at, Barb?" José asked. When Barb turned toward him, I held an imaginary gun to my head and pulled the trigger. José smiled wide.

"The Arabs." She pronounced it with a hard A, as in A-Rabs. "The virus was concocted by the Feds to wipe out the A-rab population but first they had to test it out on someone, right?" She didn't intend for us to answer.

"Sure, right," José egged her on, still smiling.

"Well, who better than the aging population? All the old fuckers in the world who gather together to drink coffee and solve all the world's problems. Who needs those guys anyway? The Feds know these guys are doing nothing but bad-mouthing the government and bringing polls down. These guys vote, right? They actually get out and vote. So, why not wipe them out by way of this virus. See if it works." She was breathless from her delivery.

"Wow," José said. He had a grim look on his face like he was actually considering what Barb said.

Barb said the Feds didn't realize how contagious the virus really was and that was how so many people ended up with it last year. Even her. Never mind that she was fifty-six and that put her at risk. She said she didn't get the vaccine because the Feds might've been targeting minorities and that was what she was, a minority. José asked her if she was Native American and she said, no, and called him a dumbass. She said, "I'm the lowest of all minorities. I am a *woman*."

José told her about the nasal mist option and Barb said that was even worse than the vaccine because they're spraying the virus directly into your brain. She asked José did he really want to put himself, as a Hispanic male, in that position? Because it was just a matter of time before the Feds would be thinning out his race as well.

I could see that José was thinking about that some more but Barb moved on. She started talking about how the last time she put anything up her nose it almost killed her.

"That was back when Coke was pure. Not like the shit they're trying to pass off as Coke these days, laced with chemicals." She held a far off note of nostalgia in her voice.

"No, I can't chance going back down that path to hell again, as beautiful a path as it was. At the end of that yellow-brick road you realize the bricks aren't really yellow, they're just painted." I pictured her waking up face down in a sewage filled gutter, reeking of someone else's piss, with a boot-print on her ass and the cartilage of her nose missing.

Where had those goddamn ear buds gone?

"No way in hell, José. No way in hell," Barb said. "I'm not getting in line for death like the Jews did. You wait and see, that's what's going to happen."

A week later José's brother died from complications from the flu. José was out for the funeral and the aftermath. Two weeks later I was moved to a new location where I sifted through my warrants and typed Martin's report for court. The report took forever. I wanted to put in a good word for him but his actions had destroyed any chance he had of redemption. His six parole violations added up to a thirteen-year, all-expenses paid trip back to the pen. Maybe longer. Okay you dumbass, I thought. It's me and you in this together to the end.

The day of Martin's sentencing, I went down to the second floor toward the enclosed walkway to the court. The route takes me past Barb. I peeked in her cube, Barb was at her computer. And she was wearing my fucking ear buds.

"Barb," I said louder than I intended.

"Shart," she said without looking up from her computer.

"Did you hear about José's brother?"

Barb looked up at me. Her eyes went from that dead jade green to a chocolate-gray and filled with tears. Her face went wrinkly and she twisted her mouth into a weird beak-like pose, like she was going to say something but couldn't form the words. A lone cigarette sat on her desk, waiting for her.

We had a moment then, her with one foot in a cast and the other in a slipper and me pissed about my ear buds. A man was dead, and I wanted to ask her where she got off taking my ear buds.

"Better be careful with those ear buds," I said. Nodding toward the wires dangling around her hunched shoulders, I whispered, "I heard they cause The Cancer."

Our Recovery

Trey and I were in a family therapy session at Recovery Village. Somewhere along the way I had turned it into a Marcus Meltdown. I hadn't intended to hijack my brother's session. I'd even apologized to the therapist for blubbering on. Of course, being the trained professional that Greg was, he raised his eyebrows into sad little arches and quietly said, "No need to apologize, Marcus. Better to get this all out on the table." Meanwhile Trey was balled up on the couch half asleep, utterly comfortable with me drowning in my emotions.

It was our fourth stint in rehab. It seemed fitting to call it *our* fourth stint, even though Trey was the one in recovery. It wasn't the first time my sexuality had come up.

"Maybe our relationship would be better if…I weren't… gay," I said.

I'd been carrying these "maybe-if-I-weren't-gay" isms around in my pocket for years. They framed my entire life. Maybe if I weren't gay, Trey wouldn't be an alcoholic. Maybe my mother would still be mentally reachable. Maybe my father wouldn't have left us. I knew that last one wasn't true. My father would've left anyway. Me being gay was just one more reason for him to frown at my mother. I still questioned my role though. I've met other homosexuals who have wondered to what depths their sexuality has contributed to the downfall of the family unit. It's a fairly common concern.

"Let's ask Trey about this," Greg said. He was a big block of a man. From his neck down, Greg reminded me of the Stretch Armstrong toy that Trey and I had spent half our childhood trying to destroy. But unlike Stretch, Greg's face was wrung out and stubbled. He kept his hair long, and tucked it behind his ears just before he said anything that might come across as direct.

Greg swiveled his chair toward Trey and rolled in closer. "Trey? What affect do you think Marcus' homosexuality has had on your life? Specifically, your alcoholism?"

"None. What do I care if he sucks dick?" Trey was practically in the fetal position by then. His face was splotched red and white. Sweat rings fanned out from his armpits.

"So, what you're saying is, Marcus' sexual orientation has had no bearing on how your life has turned out?"

"Yeah, that's what I'm saying," Trey sighed. He sat up and crossed his arms over his chest. "For the last time, I do not care if Marcus is gay, straight, or fucks donkeys."

"Well, there you have it, Marcus," Greg said.

Yeah, there I have it. Another successful therapy session for the books. A family completely healed. I wanted to scream. Why, in all the family sessions we'd sat through, had no one ever asked me how Trey's behavior had affected my life? They asked for lists in the ways his *alcoholism* had affected me but never about how his overall behavior may have shaped my life. I could've filled a few dozen pages with that list. *Dear Trey, you being a dumbass has affected me in the following ways…*

Trey was the first person to use my sexuality against me. All over a bag of potato chips. If that doesn't scream dysfunction, I'm not sure what does. I was holed up in my bedroom eating the last of Trey's potato chips while he was on the other side of my door.

"Open. The. Door. Marcus," Trey said.

Our Recovery

"Open it yourself, douchebag."

I had pushed my desk chair up under the handle of the door. Trey twisted the knob back and forth, pushed his shoulder against the door a few times, then got a running start and smashed into it. I heard him wince then go back to twisting the knob. It must've surprised him to come up on a locked door. Growing up we didn't have a single working lock in our house, not even on the front door. All the parts were there but it wouldn't latch. About every other week Mom asked Dad to fix it. He'd say, "Yeah, yeah, yeah, woman." But he never did fix it. Later, after my dad moved out, my mom tried to install a deadbolt herself but that didn't work either.

"Open the fucking door!" Trey yelled.

"Iiiiiit's open."

The way I drew out the i's, was a thing I learned from my Dad. When he mixed his nightly cocktail he'd pour rum over the ice cubes and say, "ruuuuum" drawing out the u's until he had about two-thirds of his glass full. Then he'd splash a thimbleful of Coke over the rum and say, "Coke." It was more of a quick noise in his throat than an actual word.

"I'm going to tell Mom," Trey whispered through the doorjamb. I knew he wasn't talking about me eating the last of his chips. A rock settled in my stomach, the one I'd end up carrying for the rest of my life. But right then, all I knew was that if I was going to be gay, my life was going to suck.

Trey's threat put us at a standstill. I had no countersuit yet. He was twelve and wouldn't be labeled an alcoholic for another ten years though he hit his stride well before then. During one of his brief periods of sobriety, he confessed that he'd had his first drink when he was ten. Ruuuum and Coke. Just a sip but it was enough to set his drinking in motion. By the time he went to rehab, a sip of rum and coke was what he had for breakfast. Then he'd down a twelve pack of Pabst for lunch. Dinner was rum, hold the Coke.

But this was yet undiscovered information. I moved the chair out from under the door handle and threw the bag of chips at him.

"Here, take your fucking chips, lard ass." It was the best I could come up with given the circumstances.

My gayness had surfaced only about a week before the Great Potato Chip Standoff. Trey was in my room pouring over KISS' *ALIVE!* album cover for the hundredth time since I'd bought it.

"You know Gene Simmons is what makes KISS," Trey said, goading me into our usual debate.

"Gene Simmons is nothing more than a stunt man. A dude with a long tongue."

"Yeah, but, *ALIVE* wouldn't have gone gold without Simmons."

"Answer me this, TrAnus. Who named the band? Who writes all the lyrics?"

Trey was silent. He shifted in the beanbag chair, picked something off the toe of his sock and threw it on the floor.

"What's that, Trey? Did you say Paul Stanley? I couldn't quite hear you."

"Whatever. Gene Simmons *is* KISS. The bloody mouth, the wicked tongue. That's the stuff people think about when they think about KISS." He pointed to the poster of a bloody-mouthed Simmons. Each of the four members held their place on my wall. Peter Criss was beside my bed, the others were scattered around the room.

Trey was right about Simmons being the ringleader, but I wasn't about to admit it. I pulled the album out of his hands, glanced at the cover where Simmons, Stanley, and Frehley were prominently displayed. Peter Criss was shrouded in smoke, reduced to two arms rising above a drum set. Though it was a triumphant pose, I still felt like they should've used a photo where his face was visible. I opened the album and scanned Criss' face in the group headshot. He had a quiet way about him that I was drawn to.

I had spent an inordinate amount of time staring at Criss, trying to figure a way around my feelings. Did I like cats, maybe? Did I want to be a drummer? Maybe he was just that cool. So cool that he made my dick hard. Was that possible? I wasn't about to ask around.

I waited until my face stopped burning and stinging before I turned back around to Trey. My dick was not as willing to cooperate. I pulled my shirt down to cover up the evidence.

"You know I'm right," I said. "Stanley is the brains behind the operation. Now get out of my room." I picked up my driver's training manual and hit him on the back of his head a few times to get my point across.

"Cut it out!" Trey's voice cracked mid-way through yelling at me. I considered making fun of him but didn't. He was almost out of my room and I didn't want to prolong his exit.

I closed the door behind him and listened to him plod down the hallway toward his room. His door opened and closed, his radio came on. I thought I was safe.

It was Trey's radio that did me in. I didn't hear his footsteps, didn't hear him turn the knob on my door. My eyes were closed, my ears were coursing with the thump, thump, thump of increased blood flow. I was seconds away from sweet release when Trey flung my door open. Even to this day I will sometimes try to make a deal with God to erase my memory of the way Trey's face changed as he realized what he was seeing. Peter Criss' postered face laid out across my bed, me with my dick in my hand. I could see the betrayal in my brother's eyes. He looked straight at me for a second that stretched into eternity, then bolted out of my room and down the hall. He slammed his door and cranked up the radio.

I ripped the posters off my wall, tore them up and pressed them deep into my garbage can. I cried. I bargained with God, promised to give up KISS and all things related. I packed up my sexuality and tucked it away under a mass of shame. And so began the game of my life.

The first time Trey was in rehab he was court ordered to go. He'd wrapped his car around the tree in our neighbor's front yard. I didn't know what to expect when I went to see him, what he would look like as a sober person. Turns out I had reason to worry, he looked like shit.

"You look good," I said.

Trey nodded at me. He was busy making up for ten years of lost calories, going at a fried chicken leg and a wilted baked potato like I'd never seen before.

"The food good?"

"It's alright. Nothing special."

I scanned the room. Recovery Village had a reputation for having housed a couple of radio show hosts. Local celebrities, really. I didn't see anyone I recognized, though. But it did remind me of something I'd been meaning to tell Trey.

"Hey. I heard Gene Simmons just got out of recovery."

"Yeah?" Trey wiped his mouth with the back of his hand. He'd just started in on a firm square of Jell-O sitting on a Styrofoam dessert plate. I thought he sounded hopeful.

Our Recovery

"Shit, man. Half the band has been in recovery," I said.

"Yeah?"

Trey was liquefying the Jell-O, pushing it back and forth between his teeth like he did when he was a kid. I waited for him to swallow it down. Waited for him to say something that would indicate progress toward recovery. His face was pinched up in deep thought.

"I wish I could've partied with KISS, just once before ... this," Trey said.

He eyed the room as if he hadn't taken notice of it before. The place reminded me of a prison with its dull gray cinder block walls and the dining room furniture bolted in place. The lobby was plastered with posters of white-capped mountains and calming beaches. The serenity prayer was posted about every five feet, along with the slogan, "One Day at a Time." The aged couches with their depleted cushions showed me that Trey's path was well-worn territory.

Trey picked up his chicken leg and then set it back down without eating any. He started rubbing the dry, sparse hair on the top of his head and he kept his eyes fixed on his tray.

"Those guys knew how to party." His voice was a loud whisper. It was the same voice he'd used when he was little and he would come into my room with his blanket and a pillow and tell me he was scared. He always laid down right next to my bed making it impossible for me to get out without stepping on him.

"Yeah, Trey, but they don't really know when to stop." Shit. What was I supposed to say here? I glanced around, wide-eyed and panicked. Some guy in a polo shirt with a nametag smiled at me and nodded. The asshole did not look the least bit concerned that I might've just undone Trey's sobriety with one stupid statement. The place started to bother me. They were getting my brother sober, keeping him from killing himself by way of his liver. Probably even teaching him to say he was sorry. But, they never bothered to tell me what to say to him. Or not say. If someone would've pulled me aside maybe I wouldn't have said that shit about Gene Simmons.

Trey picked up his spoon and held it out level, horizontal, with great care. He stared into the contents – likely picturing something a little more powerful than Jell-O. He was back down memory lane, like an all-star athlete recalling his game-winning touchdown.

"Did I ever tell you about the time Robby and me went down to Tijuana? Fuuuuck. Talk about your top shelf tequila."

"Trey, maybe we shouldn't talk ab—"

"—and pussy. Man, that was some goooood pussy."

And there it was. Anytime Trey and I were in the same room the gay/straight chasm would manifest itself. It sort of hung in the air between us like an aborted ghost child. I cleared my throat in warning. But he kept going.

"Robby and me were fucked up, man, and we were banging this Mexican chick, two on one when—"

"Hey! Enough. You're in rehab for Christ's sake."

Trey pushed his meal away and hung his head. He had grease smeared across his forehead. He didn't look so good then, sitting there trapped in the pain of his fate. At least Trey had the opportunity to recover, though he never did. He was lucky, really. To have the chance to recover from his disease and have everyone look upon him as a survivor and a hero for overcoming. Me – I had to live inside myself, trapped in my own little world of unacceptance.

Our Recovery

After I had made the mistake of mentioning Gene Simmons and stunting Trey's recovery, I did the only thing I could think of. I asked about my mother.

"Has Mom been around to see you yet?"

"Nah," Trey said. He waved his hand like he was shooing away a fly.

"She's probably just waiting for day pass clearance."

"Probably."

"I'll ask when I see her."

"Is she actually talking?"

I shook my head no.

Trey started chewing on his fingernails, going from one to the next in a methodical way. He'd been biting them down to the quick, drawing blood, ever since Mom went nuts. If she'd been loud about her insanity it might've been easier for all of us. But she'd gone quietly crazy all the way up to her breaking point. It had been my job to explain her behavior to Trey and pretend it was no big deal.

"Why is Mom so afraid of meteors hitting the house?"

"Oh, she probably just read about it in a Reader's Digest or some other magazine. She'll get over it."

"Mom said the government is sending her secret messages through Johnny Cash lyrics?"

"Hm. Really? I think you might've misunderstood her."

"Today when I asked about dinner Mom said something totally weird. She said, 'Keep flaming museum screen.' Then she started laughing like it was the funniest thing she'd ever said."

"That… is weird. Maybe she's been drinking."

My mother didn't drink. In fact, I'd never seen her take a single sip, not even when my dad would egg her on to join him.

Mom's breaking point came on Trey's fourteenth birthday. When we got home from school an odd smell filled the house, reminding me of Thanksgiving with all the different aromas. But something was distinctly off. Unpleasant.

Trey's eyes lit up at the sight of a cake sitting on the table. The year before Mom had completely forgotten Trey's birthday. She had moved on from worrying about meteors striking us down to thinking our neighbor lady was out to get us. (The same neighbor whose tree was later involved in a one-car accident). Mom would spend most all day peeping out the living room window over at Mrs. Humphrey's, mumbling and jotting things down in a tiny notebook. That was a tough thing to explain away.

The sight of the cake signaled to me that maybe my mother had finally come around. That we could possibly get on with being a family again.

Trey dipped a finger in the frosting, avoiding the unidentifiable globules in the center of the cake.

"Wait for Mom," I said. He smiled at me, beamed really. Probably he was thinking the same as me, taking this cake to be a good sign. Hope had the better of us that day.

I called to my mother but she didn't answer. I went around the house, stepping over piles of laundry and around stacks of used up notepads. Mom was in her bedroom, sitting on top of her perfectly made bed. She was dressed, which was a change. Jeans and a Rolling Stones t-shirt I'd seen her wear pretty regularly when she was still getting dressed. Her hair was brushed back into a ponytail. She looked good. Normal almost, except for her glassy eyed stare.

"Trey's waiting for you before he gets into the cake." I motioned for her to come with me.

Our Recovery

She grinned and patted the present beside her. It was a small package wrapped in paper that had "Joyous Noel" written all over it. Still, it was more than she'd done the year before. Way more. She edged herself off the bed and followed me down the hall.

We gathered around the kitchen table near the cake. Mom set the present on the table in front of Trey. She tapped the box then tapped Trey on the head lightly in a similar manner.

"Open it! Open it!" She started bouncing up and down and grinning so wide her eyes pressed shut.

Trey pulled the gift closer. He looked over at me. I nodded at him. "Go ahead," I said.

He ripped the wrapping paper off and set the box back down on the table. Between him and my mother I couldn't tell who was more excited.

"Open it! Open it!" Mom said again. She'd added a small clap to her bounce.

Trey eased the top off the box, just a corner of it. It did not appear, according to his face, that this particular present would be bringing him a Joyous Noel.

"What the —"

"— It's what little boys are made of. Shit and snails and puppy dog tails." My mother was in a full-blown jig by then. Laughing so hard tears streamed down her face.

Trey and I locked eyes, panicked uncertain eyes, while my mother continued to toss her word salad. I quick-stepped past her and opened the box. Two dog turds, aged white and hard, rolled together inside the box. She grabbed me by the hand and pulled me into her dance. I shook her off, harder than I meant to.

"Cake time. Time for cake!" She sang out.

Trey was crying, furiously wiping the tears off his face.

Mom lifted the cake plate off the table and started twirling around singing louder and more nonsensical. "Doggy doo-doo for my Dodo." She let go of the cake like she was flinging a Frisbee. It crashed against the floor, spewing discs of fried Spam and frosting all over the kitchen. The gelatinous glob on the top of the cake splatted against the baseboard and oozed onto the tiled floor.

I picked up the phone and dialed 911.

It was midnight by the time I heard back from the hospital. Mom was under observation in their psychiatric wing. I was to call back in the morning for more information.

"She's fucking crazy," Trey said from under his blanket.

"Something's not right. Maybe she's just upset over Dad leaving."

"He's been gone for a year, Marcus. A year."

"It takes some people a long time to get over divorce."

"She's fucking crazy."

After the conversation about my mother coming by to see Trey, I stood up to leave. I needed to get out of Recovery Village before I broke down and handed him a flask full of vodka. I made some excuse about needing to get back to the office even though it was six-thirty at night.

Trey stood up, too. "Yeah, man. Thanks for coming."

By Trey's fourth stay at Recovery Village, I knew the process well. We'd been through countless therapy sessions. I'd written a dozen lists that all started with *Dear Trey, Your alcoholism has affected me in the following ways.* I'd read the literature and learned the language of recovery. I could recite all twelve steps. I veered away from any mention of our mother. I knew which subjects to avoid that might serve as triggers for Trey. That didn't leave much to talk about.

The therapy session with Greg ended as it usually did, with the gentle chiming of an alarm he'd set. Greg turned the timer off and sent Trey on his way to a group session.

"Same time next week?" I asked.

Greg was finishing up writing on his legal pad.

"Actually, have you got just a minute, Marcus?" He closed up his pad and looked at me. I was slipping my arms into my coat, more than ready to leave.

"Well, I have some errands to run..."

"This will just take a minute."

"What's up?" I asked.

"I want to ask you a question, Marcus."

In all the sessions I'd been to, Greg had never talked to me alone. I felt sure he was going to tell me some bad news about Trey. A relapse I hadn't caught. Or, shit, something I'd done wrong that'd caused Trey to sneak a drink or two hundred.

Greg tucked his hair behind his ears. Yes, I had definitely fucked up somewhere along the way.

"In all the time you've been coming here, has Trey ever once asked how you're doing?"

"Well, no. But he's in recovery, he's probably got a lot of shit on his plate right now."

"Okay. How about when he's not in recovery? Does he ask you about your life then?"

"I don't see him much," I said.

Greg was silent. It was a therapy trick I knew well; remain quiet and let the other person fill in the silence with a stream of consciousness. We waited each other out for a few long seconds, until I couldn't take it anymore.

"Trey doesn't ever ask how I'm doing. He's an addict. He doesn't care about anything but his addiction," I said. I'd read that in the literature, figured it was a safe thing to repeat to Greg.

"Maybe so." He shrugged.

We dipped back into silence but this time I didn't wait long to break it.

"What's your point?"

"My point is that it may be time for you to stop coming to these sessions."

"What? Just give up on him? That doesn't seem like a good idea."

"No, no, no. I'm not suggesting you give up on Trey. Maybe just stop trying to make him responsible for keeping you whole."

It was my turn to shrug. My brother wasn't capable of brushing his own teeth, how could he possibly be responsible for keeping me 'whole'?

"Look, Greg, I'm not sure what you're trying to get at here, and I probably should get going."

"Marcus. All the time you spend running back and forth between Trey and your mom, it isn't helping anyone. Least of all you. The only way your brother has a chance at getting better is if you let go of him."

I started to cry. Hard enough that I had to sit down on Greg's couch again. Greg rolled his chair over to me and stretched a box of tissues out in my direction. Several minutes went by before I could speak.

"I wouldn't even know what to do with myself," I said.

"Go fuck a giraffe. Or an elephant. Your choice," Greg said.

His humor caught me off guard. Probably another therapist trick for defusing a crying jag. Still, I laughed.

Our Recovery

"You know what I mean. Go. Live. Your mom and your brother need to sort their own lives out."

"Yeah, how likely is it they'll actually accomplish that?"

"I'd say the prognosis is grim. But you don't have to suffer their fates with them."

I went home. I didn't bother to put any lights on, just sat on the couch mulling over what Greg said. Eventually I dozed off. When the sun started to rise I got up and put KISS' *ASYLUM* on the turntable. When *I'm Alive* came on, I cranked the stereo all the way up and sang along. Then, I called Greg's office and left a message on his answering machine.

"I settled on the giraffe," I said. "The elephant was a little out of my league."

Drive-By Places

I'm scrounging around the bushes in the front yard trying to find where Jimmy left my skateboard when Mrs. Rosa yells from across the street. "Hola! Guero!" I consider pretending I don't hear anything, but there's really no way I could've missed her. For one, she's huge. Jimmy says she weighs as much as a bus. And second, she's got this voice that goes off like a police siren. She smiles and waves me over.

When I get to Mrs. Rosa's she keeps on smiling, but points her bent up finger at me. I never look her in the eyes, ever. According to Jimmy, Mexicans can only put a hex on you if you look them directly in the eyes. About a month after we moved in here, Mrs. Rosa's husband chewed Jimmy out royally for shooting bb's at their garbage can. He told Jimmy if he did it again he'd call the cops, that it didn't matter Jimmy was only fifteen years old, the cops would *lock his guero ass up without thinking twice.* Ever since then, Jimmy's been running his mouth about the people in our new neighborhood.

I mean, Jimmy's always telling me things that are borderline lies. Stuff like, *if you jerk your pecker too much it'll fall off right in your hand* and *holding in a fart will explode your stomach and kill you.* Most of the time I can tell he's just bullshitting me. When Dad was still around he'd laugh right along with Jimmy, but eventually he'd tell Jimmy to knock it off, then I'd know for sure Jimmy was just yanking my chain again. With Dad gone, I have to figure out the truth on my own. It doesn't seem right to ask him when he calls. Especially with Mom eyeballing me the whole time I'm on the phone with him and tapping her finger like she does when she's irritated.

Mrs. Rosa sighs and mops her face with a hanky. Before I know it's coming, she clamps her brown hand around my wrist like a soft, fleshy handcuff and leads me toward her house. She says something in Spanish. Whatever it is sounds like one long, continuous rolling "r." Usually Jimmy's the one who gets in trouble, not me. But being his younger brother makes people look at me a certain way. It's always, "Cody Dolan? You're not related to Jimmy Dolan, are you?" I don't want to own up to it anymore.

The heat of the Indian summer is getting to Mrs. Rosa. Sweat seeps through her shirt around her boobs. *Long ass boobs*, Jimmy calls them. I can see now there's no way Mrs. Rosa could hide things under them like Jimmy said. Maybe the fly swatter, but that's a pretty big maybe. Her smile is gone.

"Tu hermano!" She points at the side of the house with her free hand. And I see what has her all worked up; a whole bunch of little holes and dents in the siding where Jimmy's been at it again. She runs her finger along the siding and says something about my *hermano* being an *idiota*. If I knew Spanish I'd tell her that my brother hasn't always been an idiot. Instead, I say the only thing I know in Spanish, "Por favor."

The screen door on Mrs. Rosa's house opens wide then closes, *bang!* like a shotgun. Children spill out like ants running from water. They are yelling, "Abuela! Abuela!" and I think maybe a wild animal is chasing them or even worse, Mrs. Rosa's husband, who Jimmy calls Señor Bean Bag.

I twist my wrist and break free from her grip. I take off down the street and glimpse over my shoulder. Mrs. Rosa's where I left

Drive-By Places

her, smiling, hugging the children and patting them on their little heads with the same hands that were on me. Dirty, filthy hands, according to Jimmy. Last week he said if a Mexican touches you, your skin will turn shit brown and rot right down to the bone. Great. Now I've got that to worry about.

I slow to a walk and catch my breath. I go past the boarded up windows at Cinema Six, past the rusted out Dodge sitting in Shooter's parking lot and into Mobley Park. Near the swings, some old, long-haired dude is hanging around sucking on a cigar. He's probably the *deranged lunatic* Jimmy told me about, the one who gives kids candy if they let him push them on the swings. He's not as bad as Jimmy described him. Yeah, his hair is greasy but he's got both his eyes. He's skinny and tired looking. Or maybe just sad.

When the guy sees me, he nods. He balances his cigar on the picnic table with the ash end hanging off, then reaches into his coat pocket. I wonder what kind of candy he's got. But, he doesn't ask to push me on the swings. Doesn't offer me any candy. What he's got is birdseed in a baggie. After a few tries, he gets the bag open and throws the seeds on the ground in front of him. So much for that. I'm not going to sit around and watch some old dude feeding birds all day. Especially not when I might have an infected wrist.

At home, I get the sink water so hot that it burns my hands. I scrub myself all the way up to my elbows, then rinse, repeat. Jimmy yells, "Are you taking a bath in there or what?" His voice is so loud it's like he's standing in the bathroom with me. I can't tell Jimmy what happened. He'll just crack on me some more. And laugh at me.

I make it through dinner, two hotdogs straight out of the package. When I get into bed I check myself with the flashlight. Click on. No dirt stains, nothing contagious looking. Click off. Click on. Still nothing. Click off. I do this until Jimmy says, "Give it a fucking rest, will ya?" He only used to use the F-word when he was sure Mom couldn't hear him. Now he says it all the time. As soon as Jimmy starts sleep-breathing, I check one last time then try to sleep.

Behind my closed eyes, Mrs. Rosa is pointing and pacing. Rolling her eyes and her "r's". Then she sees me and runs over. Her skirt flaps in the breeze and wraps around me like a cocoon. She hugs me and presses me against her boobs where it's warm and smells like melted butter and vanilla. In my dream, Dad's standing on Mrs. Rosa's porch staring off into the distance. He doesn't have a shirt or shoes on. I call out to him but Mrs. Rosa's skirt is wrapped around me so tight I can't get out any words.

I wake up sweaty. The sun is streaming through my blinds like fog. Dad used to say it was *froggy* outside instead of foggy. That used to make Jimmy laugh. I said it the other day and Jimmy just kept on reading the back of the cereal box like he could care less. Am I even allowed to think about Dad anymore?

My head feels heavy. Saturdays I have all day to remember things. Sometimes I can smell a memory, like the grass after Dad mowed or the newspaper after he read it a thousand times. When the scent fades it takes the memory with it. Today, I don't smell anything except cat litter left over from the last family who rented this place.

I'm practically back to sleep when a fly clinks against my window, half-dead, like he's lost his mind and can't remember how his wings work. He makes a full circle on the windowsill,

100

stops, rubs his hands together, then goes back around in a circle. He drags his body to the window and clinks against it trying to get out again. I wonder how many times he's going to do that before he figures out he's not going anywhere.

I head to the kitchen, careful to tiptoe as I go past Mom's room. Her door is closed again. In the kitchen, Jimmy's got the fridge open and he's drinking straight out of the milk carton, like we're not supposed to.

"What?" he says without looking at me.

"What, what?"

"What are you staring at?"

"I'm not staring."

Jimmy swigs the milk, puts the cap back on, but not all the way. The fridge door closes on its own. He tucks a cigarette behind his ear and pushes the screen door open wide. The bang it makes when it closes behind him reminds me of Mrs. Rosa. I check my wrist, my hands. Still nothing. I need the ointment Mom puts on me whenever she doesn't want me to get an infection but I don't want to go to her room and ask for it. I decide to make a piece of toast with orange marmalade on it. Mom's the only one I know who likes orange marmalade. I carry it upstairs on a paper plate and knock real quiet.

Nothing. No response.

I stand there staring at the square of toast smeared with the sickly looking jelly. I should just throw it away. Leave her alone. Instead I go in. She's lying in bed on her side with the covers crumpled up all around her. Her eyes are open and she's staring without blinking. Like a dead person.

"I brought you some toast."

She doesn't say anything. Doesn't move.

Her stomach goes up and down a little with each breath. She's not dead. I don't know whether to stay or go. Her face, which used to tell me what I should do, doesn't tell me anything. I rest the plate on her nightstand and go back to my room. The fly is just lying there on his back, his little arms and legs folded over one another.

Of course, I forgot to get the ointment.

The next morning when I get up Mom is in the kitchen making pancakes. She's humming along with the radio, swaying some whenever she flips a pancake. She sets a plate in front of me and winks. "Sweet boy," she says. I can't even remember the last time I had pancakes. Or saw Mom wink.

The thing about these kinds of days is that I always think Mom's back for good. Like I'll come home from school and she'll be in the kitchen whipping up a casserole from the recipe book that all the scraps of paper fall out of. Or she'll take my face in her hands—which I used to hate—and tell me how I look exactly like her brother, the one who died right before I was born. But by the time I get home from school she's usually back in bed, and I'm back to eating hotdogs out of the package.

Jimmy comes in and plops into the chair *with all the grace of an ox*, as Dad used to say. He pours yesterday's coffee into his juice cup and slugs it down behind Mom's back. He makes the "shhh" sign at me. Mom slides a plate of pancakes in front of Jimmy without looking at him, like a waitress in a diner too busy to be bothered.

Last week, when Pastor Warren came by to check on Mom, I overheard Mom say she could hardly stand the sight of Jimmy anymore because he was starting to look like Dad. Pastor Ward drives all the way over from Westgrove every other week to give

Drive-By Places

Mom a sermon. This last time he said something like, "You need to practice forgiveness, Corinne. Begin the healing process. You're just going to keep suffering until you do."

Right after Pastor Warren left and Mom went back to bed, Jimmy came home. He said, "What did that douchebag want?"

I told Jimmy what Pastor said about forgiveness then asked him what the suffering part meant.

"What do you think it means, dip shit?"

"Is Mom sick or something?"

"You really are stupid, aren't you?"

"C'mon, Jimmy."

"No. She's not sick. She's still pissed off at Dad for dumping us. If he hadn't decided to run out on us like he did, we wouldn't be living here in Shitsville having to dodge low-life Mexicans all the fucking time."

I don't ask anymore about it.

Jimmy *is* starting to look like Dad, especially now that his mustache is coming in. Same smile. Same smirk whenever he's trying to pull one over on you. And, the same glare whenever Mom pisses him off. Lately he's even started waving his hand at me like Dad used to do when the answer was no. Pretty soon Jimmy'll probably just stop answering me, too. If you ask me, being ignored is way worse than hearing no all the time.

Jimmy loads his pancake up with too much syrup and crams about half of it into his mouth. He pushes his plate away and makes a face.

He says, "These aren't cooked all the way."

Mom's shoulders bow and her head hangs. Her face looks like a mannequin face in the Penney's store window. Like she's trapped inside herself, frozen, back in a trance. I shoot Jimmy a look but he doesn't notice. He's already up and halfway to the door when Mom breaks out of her statue position and gets right in front of him, blocks him.

"Who do you think you are?" she shrieks. Her lips are thin, colorless. Her eyebrows are white-hot streaks on her face.

"Who do *you* think *you* are?" he yells back at her.

I can't swallow the pancake crowding up in my throat.

Mom pinches the back of Jimmy's neck and steers him away from the door. Forks and knives and pans clang around as she makes her way toward the stove, screaming.

"If you don't like my pancakes you can make your own goddamn pancakes! Do I make myself clear?"

I've never heard her cuss before. Tears race down her cheeks. A chunk of her hair comes loose and starts bobbing over her forehead. With her free hand she slaps a spatula against the counter and breaks it clean in half. Jimmy's crying and trying to pry Mom's fingers off the back of his neck, which is turning a weird red and white color.

Mom grabs Jimmy by the wrist and holds his hand out toward the stove. The burner is still on. The little blue flames stand at attention waiting for Mom to feed them. Jimmy breathes through his teeth and pushes against Mom. Even though they're practically the same size and Jimmy's pushing against her with everything he's got, he can't break free. Mom steps closer to the stove.

"Mom! Stop!" I scream. She freezes and releases her grip, but she still looks like she wants to kill Jimmy. Jimmy's bawling and shaking. I bolt out the front door and run down the street. The concrete tears at my bare feet. My lungs burn each time I breathe. My head throbs. I slow to a jog and suck in the cool fall air. Somewhere in the night, summer vanished.

Drive-By Places

I go around the block and wind up outside at the edge of Mrs. Rosa's lawn. The front door is open. I see her in the kitchen in an apron, moving back and forth, almost dancing. She stops, turns in my direction. Her face breaks into a wide flat smile. I don't move.

I stare at her through the screen that separates us. Mrs. Rosa and her husband stand together. His hands circle around her. These thick, strong hands pull her into him. He leans his massive head down toward her and pecks her cheek, gentle like I saw Dad do to Mom before. Before Mom gave up. Before Jimmy became an idiot. Before Dad dumped us. I realize Jimmy's right about one thing, none of us would be the way we are if Dad hadn't left.

Fuck Dad.

I spit on the lawn and turn toward home. I've got nowhere else to go.

Happy Birthday, Jasmine

The day before I turn fourteen the protective services lady comes to Momma's house to take Deandra and me away. At first I don't recognize her. She's just a shadow outside the screen door. You know how sometimes it's like that when the sun shines exactly a certain way and all you can make out is a person's shape. Her shape is hunched and bony. When she steps closer I see her flat, streaked hair hanging down to her shoulders like heavy drapes, and her badge dangling on a string around her neck. I realize she's the same lady who came to my school the week before and asked me a hundred questions.

She looks different on the porch. Probably because she's standing opposite Momma. And because of the way the sun's throwing Momma's shadow out the front door onto her. Momma, with her wild hair and big round body, looks like a ball pumped too full with air. Especially when she's fixing to whoop somebody's behind and she gets to huffing and puffing and goes short of breath. When the lady comes that day, that's exactly what Momma does.

The week before when the lady comes to my school and they call for me at the office, I'm in gym class. I've never been called to the office before so I think somebody died. Momma maybe. But no, it's just some tired-face lady, smiling and winking at me every couple of seconds while she tells me she's from the Department of

Family and Children's Services. Her eyes are a funny blue color that make me feel like I'm staring into an empty hole when I look at her. Out in the hallway she starts in on me about Deandra's daddy.

She asks, *Jasmine, does Deon Wilkes live at your house?*

At first I don't know who she's talking about because we call him Butter. Everybody on the street calls him Butter. When he first started showing up at Momma's, I asked my friend Teisha if she knew him. She did.

"Why's he called Butter?" I asked.

Teisha laughed at me, "You don't know?"

I shook my head. I like Teisha but not when she gets all superior acting.

"He's smooth. And slippery, too. Real good at making women fat. Like butter." Teisha told me he'd been coming around for her momma too.

"I guess his name's about right for him," I said. Then we laughed because what else was there to do?

In the school hallway, I look at the lady, smile back at her dull face without answering. She loses her smile a little and presses on her forehead with her index finger. She goes on, calls him 'Deandra's daddy,' like it might make a difference.

Does Deandra's daddy live at your mother's house?

I tell her, *Nobody lives at Momma's house but me, Deandra, and Momma.*

I don't tell her how Butter comes and stays a few days here and there. How things are fine at first but then he and Momma get to drinking and arguing, sometimes shoving each other around and banging against the walls. I haven't seen Butter since the last time the police came around.

Happy Birthday, Jasmine

When did you see Deandra's daddy last?

I don't answer because I don't know for sure.

She says, *Think, Jasmine. This is very important.*

I ask her if she could just talk to Deandra since he's her daddy and all.

She glares at me, makes her lips go tight. Then she gets back to smiling and says, *Let me ask you this. What if I was to tell you Deandra's daddy is in a lot of trouble?*

I say, *Okay.*

What if I was to tell you that the police are looking for him?

I say, *Okay.*

That he did something so bad that he can't ever be around children again?

I don't say anything.

She says, *See, Jasmine? This is important.*

After a minute I say, *I haven't seen him in a couple of weeks. Maybe longer.*

She smiles in a different way then, like Granny smiles after I finally tell her the truth. She doesn't ask me anything more, just pats my hand and tells me to go on ahead back to Ms. Hayes' class.

Later that night I ask Deandra if she got called down to the office, too.

Deandra nods but doesn't look up from petting her cat. It's not really her cat, just some stray that comes around begging, but she named him so she thinks he's hers. It climbs into Deandra's lap and digs its claws into her legs trying to get comfortable. I wonder if Deandra knows the cat is just hoping for some food, that he doesn't really care about her.

Since this is about Deandra's daddy and not mine, I don't ask her anything more. I wish the lady had been asking about my daddy. That would've been easy to answer. Deandra's quiet the rest of the night and I don't know what to do with myself. Nobody said I *can't* tell Momma, but I don't. I know Momma will ask me from now until forever what that lady said to me. A lot of times Momma doesn't listen, and I sit there while she gets red-hot and screams. Then she starts crying and saying her life is too hard, and why can't things be easy for once? She always ends up wiping her eyes and saying, "Thank God for my girls," and hugging us tight, making us promise we'll be good girls and stay out of trouble. Her hugs are the softest place I've ever been.

That night when Deandra isn't talking to me and I'm not talking to Momma, I go to bed thinking about the protective services lady and all her questions. I wonder if what Teisha told me is true, if they really ask questions over and over again until you say something you don't mean, then use what you said against you to haul you away to some foster care house and never let you see your momma again. Teisha knows a lot but I'm never sure if she's right.

I find out the day I turn fourteen.

When the lady comes to Momma's house, Deandra starts whining as soon as she sees her on the front porch. The fan's going near the screen door to get us a breeze, but the only thing blowing is hot air. The lady sees us and waves, like we're going to get up. When we don't, she drops her wave and starts knocking on the door. When we still don't move, she takes to banging on the door, and frowning.

Momma's in the kitchen frying bacon and smoking a cigarette. She yells, *Answer the door.*

Dee and me are squeezed up on the couch, hanging onto each other, not knowing what to do.

Happy Birthday, Jasmine

I say, *It's for you, Momma.*

She asks, *Who's at my door?* Then comes out from the kitchen and goes to the screen.

The protective services lady says, *D-FACS.*

Momma says, *D what?* Like she doesn't know.

Jennifer Wayne from the Department of Family and Children Services.

Momma squinches up her eyes. The ash from her cigarette falls on the carpet. After a minute she says, *What do you want?*

Ms. Wayne says, *We need to ask you some questions regarding Deon Wilkes.*

He don't live here.

We already know he does.

The hell he does.

Are you calling your daughter a liar, ma'am?

Momma turns her face slow toward us. Her eyes go small and black, dart between me and Deandra, then back at Ms. Wayne. For a second I don't want Ms. Wayne to leave without me. Deandra's grabbing me even tighter now, tearing up. And I'm thinking this is all her fault because Butter's *her* daddy and why couldn't he just done like *my* daddy had and never come around on account of being dead.

Momma says, *It don't matter what Jasmine or Deandra told you. He ain't been here. He don't live here.*

Ms. Wayne says, *Miss Mona. Do you really want to play this game?*

I ain't playing no game.

You are well aware of Mr. Wilkes' criminal charges.

And?

You know you were to call the police if he came back around here.

He ain't been around here, I told you that.

111

I know for a fact he's been here.

Ms. Wayne stares right at me, mean and hateful. She turns her stupid, sour face back to Momma. She says, *The girls need to pack a few things and come with me.*

Momma says, *My girls are staying right here with me.*

Deandra begins howling in my ear in between hiccupping and squeezing me. I'm saying *Shhhh* and *Hush,* and keeping my eye on the situation. Momma straightens her back, cocks her head, presses one hand in the crook of her heavy hip. Her cigarette's about burnt down to her fingers. I can hear the bacon crackling and popping in the kitchen.

Ms. Wayne's still on the porch, not moving, maybe making up her mind what to do next. She reaches for the screen door handle, real slow, without taking her beady eyes off Momma.

Now Momma's eye to eye with her, just the screen between them. Momma snaps the lock on the door. Even I know that lock doesn't work anymore. She says, *Ain't no baby-stealing bitch coming in my house.*

Ms. Wayne takes her hand off the door. She says, *We can do this the easy way or the hard way.* She nods at the police waiting by the curb. I see him out the window. Around the neighborhood he's known as Skunk. He sweats so much you can smell him before you see him. Ol' Skunk never busted anybody, as far as I know.

Momma says, *You go on, get the police. Have him come tell me what I done wrong.*

Ms. Wayne sighs, *Fine, Ms. Mona, Fine.* She motions with her arm and up comes Skunk with a hat too small for his fat pig head. He stands behind Ms. Wayne, sucks in his gut and taps his sausage link fingers on his gun handle. Sweat stains his arm pits.

Skunk clears his throat and says firmly, *Ma'am, open the door.*

Happy Birthday, Jasmine

Momma puffs up her chest, every inch of her big body's gone firm. Her jaw is working and her hands are balled up in tight fists. Deandra's wimpering. I'm holding my breath to keep the trouble from coming. Both of us watch to see what's going to happen now.

Skunk grabs the door handle, flings the door open and pushes in front of Ms. Wayne. He grabs tight to his gun handle and his club, his basketball gut hanging over his pants.

Ms. Wayne trails in behind him. She says, *This'll all be cleared up soon enough with the Judge, but for now we've got to get the girls somewhere safe. It's just temporary.*

Nobody sees what I see on Momma's face just then. She's gone, switched over to the same eyes she had when she found out my daddy had died.

Smoke curls across the ceiling from the kitchen. The house goes quiet from Deandra finally hushing up and from the fight that's hanging in the air. It's the kind of quiet you hear just before a wave crashes down on itself. Or just before thunder claps and lightning zaps the sky. You know it's coming but it still makes you jump when the noise finally breaks the silence.

Ms. Wayne says to me and Deandra, *Girls go get yourselves a couple of changes of clothes. Your toothbrushes. Clean panties. Whatever else you can fit in your pillowcases.*

Skunk's eyes are roaming around Momma's place, his face in a frown. He isn't paying attention to the tide rolling in. Ms. Wayne's got her back to Momma while she's going on about the things we need and don't need packed.

Momma breaks the quiet with a hard and fast fist to the side of Ms. Wayne's head. She jumps on top of Ms. Wayne, straddling her with her legs and they go down. There's a thump and a grunt as Momma lands another punch, this time right in Ms. Wayne's mouth. Blood comes quick to her lip. Momma yells, *Ain't nobody going nowhere.*

Ms. Wayne's flat on the carpet, thrashing around and holding the side of her head where the blood is coloring her yellow hair red.

The women are screaming and tussling and Skunk's just standing there with his face hanging open. Deandra's all but on top of me in my lap like a baby. A TV commercial's blasting, the bacon's burning and I'm wondering what to do. Do I help Momma, slap Deandra, turn off the stove, pack my panties, or run.

I can't move.

Skunk jimmies his club free from his belt and starts whacking Momma. Each time he strikes, Ms. Wayne groans underneath her. Momma's like a wild animal, grunting and screaming. Skunk's sweating more now, big drops sliding down the side of his thick skull. He gets his club up under Momma's chin and chokes her until her eyes roll back into her head and she falls off Ms. Wayne. Momma makes a low growling noise then goes silent.

Skunk's calling on his police radio saying, *I need immediate back-up. A suspect is down and D-FACS worker is injured.*

He asks Ms. Wayne, *You okay?*

Ms. Wayne's panting and gasping and pulling her badge from around her neck. She sits up. She's missing some hair on the side of her head. She gets up on one knee, nods and stands.

Skunk says, *Get the girls out of the house.*

I pry Deandra off me and tell her, *Come on.*

Deandra won't go until Skunk pushes her out the front door. Ms. Wayne's behind us, carrying her hair and her badge in her hand. She's gasping for breath and wiping tears away.

114

Happy Birthday, Jasmine

When we get to the foster care house we smell like four-day-old grease and sweat and our faces are messed up from crying. We get introduced to the foster lady, a skinny, gray-haired lady who doesn't stop smiling. She acts like she doesn't notice how bad we look and just goes on and shows us to our bedroom. Then she feeds us some hard cookies and Kool-Aid. She doesn't ask anything but our names and we don't tell her anything more than Deandra and Jasmine. She tells us her name, Loretta Roberts.

She says, *Maybe you girls would like to watch TV awhile before dinner?*

Deandra and I go sit on the edge of the couch. We don't say anything, just stare at the TV like Ms. Loretta wants us to. I count six crosses hanging on the wall behind the TV. Different sizes but all wooden. One with a bible verse on it so small I'd have to get up to read it. The couch is firm like nobody ever sits on it.

It's cold in here, Deandra says.

When Mr. Roberts comes home we eat meatloaf and he and Ms. Loretta tell us about their grown kids and all the kids they've had come to their house over the years. *Kids with family troubles just like you,* Ms. Loretta says. Deandra peeks at me and I know what she's thinking. There's no way that many kids came here with a daddy so bad he isn't allowed around, and a momma who got choked out by a police for messing up the protective services lady. But we go on and nod and eat. The food doesn't taste like Momma's, it doesn't taste like anything.

They buy us clothes for school and put us on the bus every morning until summer comes. Then they take us to the lake where we swim and then sit and eat sandwiches at a table on the grass. Dee and me lie on beach towels by the lake, listen to the water

115

splash around in small waves. The faint lap of the waves puts me to sleep.

Sometimes at night I hear Dee crying. I think about Momma, what she's doing. How we need to do what she said, be good. Stay out of trouble. Seems like Momma's the one who's got trouble, the one who needs to be good.

We see Momma every Saturday at the DFACS building. We go in a room with a chair set out in the corner where a worker sits and watches us. We get a different worker assigned to us than the one Momma jumped. The table's dirty and marked up from crayons. Momma talks quiet and sweet and tells us how much she misses us and how nice we're dressed and asks do we miss her? Kissing and hugging her isn't enough; we've got to tell her we miss her. She asks about The Roberts' and we say they're fine but we'd rather be home with her. She asks about the food every time we see her. At the first visit Deandra told Momma that Ms. Loretta makes the best sweet potato pie and that set Momma's jaw to working.

Momma tells us she's doing her treatment plan and dropping urine every time they ask her to. She tells us Butter's in jail and that we'll be home in no time. Deandra sobs and says she wants to go home with Momma now, then makes a pouty face the rest of the visit. Momma tells her she's going to be fine and we're going to be fine and we're all going to be one family again real soon. To me, Momma looks like someone let a little of the air out of her.

Momma starts skipping visits here and there. We wait for her in the room, every minute lasting an hour. First she says she's sick. Then she says she missed the bus. Every time she doesn't come we sit and wait. Deandra mopes.

Happy Birthday, Jasmine

The next time we see Momma, she says, *I ain't been feeling well lately. But I came to see my girls anyway. I had to see my girls.* She doesn't look so good. Her fingernails are dirty and her clothes are crumpled and smell.

She reaches for us, gathers us up against her so close. We smell the way her days have gone. This time Deandra goes straight past crying and makes her mad face. She doesn't even look at Momma till the end of the visit and then she starts back to her usual fussing and saying she wants to go home. I want to go home too but saying so won't help the situation.

Then Momma doesn't come for a whole month. We stop going to the DFACS building altogether on account of it takes too much time out of Ms. Loretta's schedule. We're told we'll go back as soon as they hear from Momma again. It takes all the way to my next birthday, three months almost, before we see Momma again. She's lost weight. Her big, round middle hangs lower. Her eyes droop into small pools of dark skin that have gathered since I saw her last. Her teeth are like Mr. Joe's. I haven't thought about Mr. Joe since I seen him laid up against the building outside the gas station. His empty, crinkled up eyes, his mouth gaped open like he's about to say something. Momma's got the same look on her face as him. When she talks, I hold my breath. This is some kind of birthday, again. I start crying and I can't stop. Deandra squeezes my hand under the dirty table with the crayon marks. For once she's got dry eyes.

Momma asks, *What are you all up to this weekend?*

Deandra pats my hand and says, *Momma, it's Jazz birthday tomorrow, remember? Ms. Loretta made a yellow cake with chocolate frosting. And fifteen candles.*

I go stiff waiting for Momma to snap. But, she doesn't even frown. Instead she nods her head, grins and says, *Oh, that sounds nice.*

The lady from the corner tells us our visit time's over and to say good-bye.

Momma stands up from the table, grinning wide like Joe when you throw a dime in his cup. She grabs me for a hug. I wrap my arms around her and rest my head on her shoulder. I breathe deep, search for Momma's powdery scent. I can't find it. I squeeze her tighter, bury my face in the crook of her neck, close up against her skin. She smells hot and tinny, like she's rotting from the inside out. She lets me loose so Deandra can take her turn.

Outside Ms. Loretta is waiting in her minivan. She's got balloons tied up in the back seat, all kinds of colors, one has *Happy Birthday Jasmine!* printed on it.

When we get in she says, *How'd it go?*

Deandra says, *Fine.*

I don't say anything. Just think about the yellow cake back at the Roberts' house. I already know it's going to taste like cardboard. Everything Ms. Loretta makes tastes like cardboard. And I know how the whole house is going to smell from those candles she burns all the time. How she's not going to stop stealing looks at us like we're some pitiful animals she's rescued off the side of the road. She's never going to stop smiling at us thinking that's all it's going to take to make our lives right again.

I slide the van door closed but it doesn't latch. When I try again, I slam it shut and move the whole van back and forth. Once I'm in my seat the balloons surround me and bob at my face. I tap my finger on them, one at a time. I like how they sound when I plunk at them, hollow and empty, yet full at the same time; the

Happy Birthday, Jasmine

way they fly away from me fast then float back slow. I do that all the way home.